WRANGLING WES

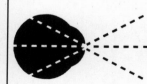

This Large Print Book carries the
Seal of Approval of N.A.V.H.

WRANGLING WES

JACQUELIN THOMAS

THORNDIKE PRESS
A part of Gale, Cengage Learning

GALE
CENGAGE Learning®

Farmington Hills, Mich • San Francisco • New York • Waterville, Maine
Meriden, Conn • Mason, Ohio • Chicago

GALE
CENGAGE Learning®

Copyright © 2014 by Jacquelin Thomas.
The Browards of Montana Series #1.
Thorndike Press, a part of Gale, Cengage Learning.

LIBRARY OF CONGRESS CATALOGING-IN-PUBLICATION DATA

Thomas, Jacquelin.
  Wrangling Wes / by Jacquelin Thomas. — Large print edition.
    pages ; cm. — (The Browards of Montana series ; #1) (Thorndike Press large print African-American)
  ISBN 978-1-4104-6836-9 (hardcover) — ISBN 1-4104-6836-4 (hardcover)
  1. African Americans—Fiction. 2. Cowboys—Fiction. 3. Montana—Fiction. 4. Large type books. I. Title.
PS3570.H5637W73 2014
813'.54—dc23   2014002804

Published in 2014 by arrangement with Harlequin Books S.A.

Printed in Mexico
1 2 3 4 5 6 7 18 17 16 15 14

Dear Reader,

Lydia Emerson arrives in Granger, Montana, with an alias and the intent to learn more about Wes Broward, a handsome cowboy. Although in town on assignment, Lydia soon discovers that romance is in the air in Big Sky Country.

In fact, there are many others who would agree with Lydia. Montana was recently ranked as one of the top romantic states, according to NBC Montana. However, there has always been a certain romanticism connected to the West. I really enjoyed writing *Wrangling Wes* because this story allowed a glimpse of the beauty of Montana through the eyes of Lydia and Wes.

Best regards,
Jacquelin

CHAPTER 1

Wesley Broward groaned loudly as he flung his right hand toward his shrilly ringing alarm clock. The sun wasn't up yet, but the small town of Granger, Montana, was already coming alive as cowboys working cattle on the BWB Ranch rode out to pasture to begin the day's work.

Getting up at 4:00 a.m. every morning to saddle a horse and trot off across the prairie was not for everybody — it definitely was not Wesley's idea of a great way to start his day. But for most cowboys it was the norm — an important part of the job they cherished.

With another groan of protest, Wesley propelled himself out of bed and padded barefoot into the bathroom. A pair of tired brown eyes stared back as he gazed at his reflection in the mirror. He brushed his teeth and then fingered his neat goatee before jumping into the shower.

Fifteen minutes later, he was dressed in a pair of faded denims, a crisp plaid shirt and cowboy boots. Wesley headed out to the main house, where his parents and grandfather lived. He was on his way to join the rest of the family for breakfast. Wesley and his siblings, Jameson and Laney, often had their meals in the main house, although they all lived on the ranch.

His parents, Steven and Gwendolyn, flourished in thirty-four years of marriage, despite town gossip that theirs was an arranged marriage, a merger between two wealthy families. Even though his parents had an unconventional courtship and marriage, they truly loved and respected one another. They shared something he had never experienced with most of the women he dated — complete and total honesty. There was always some hidden agenda.

His mother's family — the Webbs — had made its fortune breeding rare stallions. When the two families were joined, Steven and Gwendolyn Webb Broward became the two largest landowners in the state. Wesley reasoned that his parents' marriage was so successful because Gwendolyn was wealthy in her own right. She and Steven were equals.

Just as Wesley entered through the front

door of his parents' home, he heard a familiar voice holler, "Come and get it."

Amused, Wesley broke into a grin as he quickly made his way to the dining room. The cook, Rusty, had been whipping up meals for cowboys for nearly twenty years. Rusty recently celebrated his fourth year with the Broward family. His culinary skills were in high demand, and Wesley was grateful that the sixty-something-year-old man had decided to work for his family.

"Morning, y'all," Wesley greeted as he sat down across from his sister, Laney.

"Good morning, dear," his mother responded with a warm smile. "Rusty made all your favorites this morning."

Wesley grinned. "It's a good thing I brought my appetite."

He picked up a plate and loaded it with Rusty's famous sausage, egg and cheese casserole, three slices of bacon, assorted fruit and a biscuit.

"Laney and I are driving into town later this afternoon," Gwendolyn announced as she reached for her water glass. "We need to pick up our dresses for tomorrow night's gala. Have you boys picked up your tuxedoes yet?" She took a sip of ice water.

"I brought mine home last Saturday," Jameson announced as he slathered butter on a biscuit.

"I'll grab my tux and Dad's later this afternoon," Wesley stated. "Grandpa said that he's wearing the same one he bought last year." His gaze traveled to where Charles Broward sat — on one end of the table while his son, Wesley's father, sat at the head.

"I sure am," Charles confirmed. "It's clean . . . looks good as new. I'm not spending money on another tux. Y'all can bury me in it as far as I'm concerned. I intend to get my money's worth."

Wesley laughed as he helped himself to another biscuit. He loved his grandfather's sense of humor and his zest for life. At the age of eighty-four, Charles Broward was still in good health and enjoyed running cattle every now and then.

"Mama, I hope you can maneuver around all of the tourists," Jameson said. "Granger's not been the same since Laney brought home that gold medal."

Wesley felt a thread of pride snake down his spine at the mention of his sister's name. Laney was skilled in three-day eventing, a grueling sport that combined the disciplines of dressage, show jumping and cross-country, which recently earned her a gold medal in the summer Olympic Games. "I think it's a good thing," Gwendolyn responded. "Tourism has certainly picked up."

Wesley agreed. More and more visitors were flocking to the town every day, including celebrities.

Although some said that the town was a mile from heaven, it was in reality located about one hundred miles north of the capital city. Granger had a population of two thousand. The only reason anyone had ever heard of Granger was because of his family's financial standing. The Broward family was named the wealthiest ranchers in the state of Montana.

Gwendolyn wiped her mouth on the edge of her napkin. "Granger is a beautiful place to live and raise a family. The town has a rich history and much more to offer. It's a hidden gem, in my opinion."

He studied his mother for a moment. She was gentle, serenely wise and beautiful. She was also one of the top horse breeders in the country.

Gwendolyn met his gaze and smiled warmly. "Mayor Thorne told me that business has been booming for downtown Granger. Even our local grocery store is experiencing a boom in business. Laney's success as an Olympian has contributed to Granger's long-term economic stability."

Frowning into his glass of orange juice, Jameson uttered, "I can't believe you're okay with a bunch of strangers coming into town and corrupting everything our community has built here."

"Stop being so negative, Jameson," Laney interjected, a hint of irritation in her voice. "This is a good thing. Mama is right. Tourism is a good thing because it brings in money for the town. I certainly don't see anything wrong with that."

"I don't, either," Charles stated. "Now, what I don't like is the sudden influx of celebrities coming to Granger and wanting to turn it into some type of playground for the rich and famous. I heard some singer wanted to buy the Triple K Ranch and remodel it into some fancy mansion."

"They were talking about it on the news last night," Wesley contributed. "It's not going to happen though. The owners have decided not to sell the place."

"Good," Jameson stated.

"Tomorrow is the big night," Charles announced. "The annual Cowboy Auction." His gaze traveled over to his grandson, and he said, "Wes, I'm sure you're gonna bring in a pretty penny. You being the 'Most Eligible Rancher' and all."

"Grandpa, I wouldn't even participate if it

12

wasn't for charity," Wes responded smoothly, keeping his face void of emotion. His family cosponsored the annual gala fundraiser for the Granger Farmland Preservation Society.

"You and Jameson usually bring in the most money," Gwendolyn interjected. "The Granger Farmland Preservation Society appreciates all you do for the fundraiser."

Jameson grunted in response.

She released a soft sigh. "I know how much you all hate participating in the auction, but can you please remember that this is for charity?"

"I'm actually thinking about putting myself on the auction block," Charles announced. "I'm pretty sure I can still fetch a dollar or two."

Wesley laughed. It had been three years since the death of his grandmother May. He knew that his grandfather was lonely and some female companionship might be just what he needed, even for one night.

"Maybe you should, Grandpa. Jameson and I will need some stiff competition tomorrow night."

"Actually, Grandpa, you should participate in the auction," Jameson agreed. "Then I can sit this one out."

His mother shook her head. "There's

room for all three of you. Jameson, why do we have to go through this every year?"

"I know it's for charity, Mom," he said, "but I hate being on display like a piece of meat."

Wesley stole a glance at his mother, who was silently studying his sister. He noted the intense but secret expression on Laney's face. Something was going on with her — something she was not ready to share with any of them.

"You're awfully quiet, Laney," Gwendolyn stated. "Are you okay?"

"I'm fine."

It was apparent to Wesley that his mother was not convinced. "Why don't you go out for a morning ride? It might lift your mood," he suggested.

In truth, he was not convinced, either. "I'll ride with you," Wesley offered. Maybe if it were just the two of them, Laney might open up to him.

"Thanks, Wes, but I really don't feel like riding," Laney responded as she rose to her feet. "I think I'll just go down to the office. I need to check on the medical supplies and see what needs to be replenished. I know that we are out of some stuff."

"What's going on with Laney?" Wesley inquired after she left the room. "She hasn't

14

seemed like herself in days." In fact, he thought Laney looked a little pale.

Jameson agreed. "I've noticed it, too. Maybe it's because she's no longer in the limelight as much. She could be going through a sort of media withdrawal."

"I don't think that's what it is," Gwendolyn stated. "But I know my daughter. Something is bothering her."

He had never seen Laney look so troubled. Wesley had no idea what was going on with his sister, but he intended to find out.

Lydia LaSalle . . . LaSalle . . . she repeated over and over in her mind. Her feet slowed as she neared the front desk of the hotel.

"Hello, my name is Lydia LaSalle and I have a reservation." Her voice sounded a pitch higher than she would have liked.

The hotel clerk, a young woman, glanced up from the computer monitor, smiling warmly. "Welcome to the Granger Hotel, Miss LaSalle."

Lydia set her iPhone on the counter and pulled a wallet out of her purse.

"We've reserved the Emerald Suite for you."

She smiled. "Thank you." Lydia relaxed as she accepted the room key from the clerk. She worried that the fake driver's license would not pass the woman's scrutiny, but everything was working according to plan.

"I hope you will find your stay with us an enjoyable one," the front-desk clerk said.

"I'm sure I will," Lydia responded. She put away her wallet as she walked toward the elevators.

"Miss LaSalle . . ."

It took a moment for Lydia to remember that the woman was addressing her. She turned around to find the desk clerk holding up her cell phone. She had been caught off guard — something Lydia could not allow to happen again.

"Oh, my goodness," she murmured. "Thanks so much. I would be completely lost without my phone."

She had checked in the hotel as Lydia LaSalle but her real name was Lydia Emerson. As far as the people in this small town were concerned, she was a wealthy heiress on vacation.

Lydia tipped the bellhop twenty dollars after he set the three pieces of designer luggage inside her suite. She had just recently arrived in town, but she had a to-do list a mile long.

As soon as she was alone in the suite, Lydia ran into the bedroom and dived into the king-size bed.

"Ooh . . . this feels wonderful." Although she traveled a lot, Lydia had never stayed in a room as extravagant as this one, which was decorated in rich jewel-tone colors and dark mahogany.

"Okay, enough being silly," she whispered. "I have a lot to do, so I need to get unpacked."

She picked up a suitcase.

"Ow!"

She hopped on her left foot and clutched at the bruised toes on her right one. Shooting a furious glare at the bolted-down table, Lydia limped her way over to the king-size bed.

She laid the suitcase down on the bed.

With her aching toes throbbing in concert with her beating heart, Lydia opened it and began removing the contents.

She moved forward, encountering the average-size walk-in closet. Lydia hung up the gown she'd planned to wear to the upcoming charity function. She had only dreamed of wearing a couture creation like this and never expected it to come true.

After unpacking, Lydia sat down on the edge of her bed. She picked up her cell phone and dialed.

"Hey, girl . . ."

She smiled at the sound of her best

friend's voice. "Jasmine, I just wanted to let you know that I made it to Granger." They'd met during Lydia's first week in Los Angeles and had become fast friends.

"I can't believe you're in Montana. With your job, I figured you'd be taking trips to places like Europe or some exotic island."

"Not this time around."

"Take lots of pictures for me. I doubt I'll ever visit Montana."

Lydia laughed. "It's actually quite pretty here. The mountains, the lakes and miles of gorgeous blue sky."

"Really? Maybe I should come visit."

"You'd be bored after a couple of days, Jasmine. While it's beautiful here, there is nothing but a bunch of ranches, cattle and cowboys — none of which is of interest to you."

"You're right," her friend responded. "I really don't know how you're going to survive these next few weeks. You're a city girl."

"I'll manage," Lydia responded with a chuckle. "I'm sure I'll have enough work to keep me busy."

"Well, make sure to try and have some fun. Don't work too hard."

Lydia laughed. "And you get some work done. Cut back on the fun."

She hung up with Jasmine and called her mother next.

As expected, the call went to voice mail. "Mama, I just wanted you to know that I'm in Montana for business. I'm going to be here for a few weeks. Call me when you get a minute." Her mother worked odd hours at the post office in Syracuse, her hometown. She hoped to make enough money one day to convince her mother to retire. The woman had worked hard all of her life. Lydia wanted her mother to take a moment to relax.

Lydia decided to have lunch delivered to her room.

While she waited for her food to arrive, Lydia sat down on the sofa and pulled a folder out of her leather tote.

A photograph fell into her lap.

Wesley Broward was a very handsome man, indeed. Thirty years old and single, although it was rumored that he had left a string of broken hearts all over the Mountain States. Lydia could clearly understand why women were so drawn to him — those sexy brown eyes and smooth complexion except for the neatly trimmed mustache and goatee. According to her notes, he stood six feet tall and was well-fit and muscular. Lydia knew that Wesley wasn't much of a society man, but someone with his wealth could not completely escape the attention of gossip columns and news magazines.

She was looking forward to meeting the Broward family, but Lydia was especially excited at the prospect of getting to know Wesley. Her eyes traveled to his face.

It was so easy to get lost in those intense eyes of his, she cautioned herself. Lydia reminded herself that she was not in Granger to fall in love with a cowboy. As soon as her work was finished, Lydia intended to return to Los Angeles.

Wesley strolled outside after everyone had finished eating breakfast. It was time to get his day started. He paused on the porch, allowing the subtle warmth from the morning sun to embrace him.

"I guess you'll be adding another broken heart to your list after tomorrow night," Jameson said as he stood beside Wesley.

"Actually, I have no intentions of getting involved with my date. It's too much trouble," he responded. "What about you? Women in Granger have been trying to tie you down for years."

"Not for the right reasons," Jameson said. His lips curved upward. "And I have enough sense to leave it at one date. But then again, no one has ever tossed their underwear on-stage to me."

Recalling the incident, Wesley burst into laughter. "I forgot all about that. The auction last year did get a little wild. That auction was the cowboy's equivalent of a rock concert. I felt like a rock star."

Jameson chuckled. "All right, *Rock Star . . .* let's get our horses and take a ride."

They made their way to the stables and quickly saddled their horses.

Minutes later, the cool, April morning stillness was punctured by the slapping of saddle leather, the jingling of spurs and the rhythmic beat of horses' hooves on the soft ground as Wesley and Jameson rode their horses down the road toward the pasture where the workers had taken the cattle to graze.

"I'm going to ride around the perimeter," Wesley stated. He usually performed a check every other day to make sure there were no broken or stretched wires, broken posts, fallen trees or branches on the fence line.

There was a time when he was excited to be outside with the cattle, but things had changed lately. He was restless.

Ranching was in his blood. Wesley was born into the lifestyle, but there was a longing — a longing to try something new. He just had no idea what he wanted to do. It wasn't what he considered a burning desire, but an itch to explore the possibilities was severe enough to stay in the forefront of his mind.

His mother considered his restlessness as a sign to settle down with a wife and have a family of his own. Wesley wasn't exactly opposed to the idea of marriage; it was finding the right woman that presented a challenge. He had already decided that he would have to look outside Granger for a wife. Most of the women he had come in contact with seemed to have more of an interest in the family wealth than in him. His parents were both well-off when they met and married. Wesley believed he would have to find a woman who already had financial security to take as his mate.

He valued honesty above all other qualities. The rumor mill had him painted as a ladies' man, but while he enjoyed the attention of women, he had no patience when it came to manipulation and deceit.

Lydia turned around slowly as she eyed her reflection in the full-length mirror. The dress really was gorgeous and cost more than what she made in a month. Thankfully, she had not been the one to foot the bill for it.

In keeping her true identity a secret, it was important that she dress the part, as well. She was about to mingle with some of Montana's wealthiest residents. Lydia inhaled deeply, and then exhaled.

Please don't let me make a fool of myself, she prayed.

This should be easy, Lydia silently reasoned. After all, she had been pretending most of her life. Her father left when she was young and appeared sporadically throughout her teen years. The story Lydia told to her friends growing up was that his absence was because he worked overseas. No one ever knew how hard it was for Lydia and her mother to make ends meet.

At one point, her mother worked two jobs, leaving Lydia to fend for herself. When she started high school, her mother landed employment with the post office where she was now a supervisor.

Lydia shook away thoughts of the past. She wanted only to focus on the present, and right now she had a gala to attend.

She grabbed her clutch purse and made her way downstairs to the ballroom where the gala was being held.

Shortly after Lydia's arrival, Wesley

strolled into the ballroom alongside his brother, causing a stir among the ladies in attendance.

She was careful to stay out of sight. Lydia wanted a chance to observe Wesley without his knowledge.

He was very handsome, and from his body language, it was obvious that Wesley knew that he looked good.

He was well aware of the magnetism he exuded. Lydia was sure of it. She was by no means blinded by his appeal, but such an attraction could prove disastrous. Lydia was determined to do exactly what she came to do — nothing more. The last thing she intended to do was get involved with a cowboy. She couldn't imagine anything they would have in common.

She took note of his parents when they arrived with daughter Laney. The Browards were a stunning family. Steven stood tall like his sons; he was bald with a graying beard. His wife, Gwendolyn, was a tall woman with a medium brown complexion and intelligent eyes that missed nothing. Wesley's sister had an athletic build, although she moved about gracefully. She wore her long brown hair straight.

The patriarch, Charles Broward, entered the room within minutes of the rest of the family, smiling and even flirting with a few of the women. He was still a handsome man with distinctive blue eyes despite his advanced age.

Lydia noticed a couple of females staring in her direction and whispering. Most likely, they were discussing her. After all, she was the interloper. She supposed this was due to Granger being a small town with a population of about two thousand.

She lifted her chin, meeting their curious gazes straight on. Lydia gave them a tiny smile before walking toward the bar. Lydia caught sight of Wesley coming toward her and quickly changed directions. She was not ready for him to take notice of her.

"Your dress is stunning," a young woman complimented. She was standing directly in Lydia's path.

"Thank you. I love the color of your gown," Lydia responded with a smile. "That shade of blue is a favorite of mine." After a brief pause, she added, "Hi, I'm Lydia."

"It's nice to meet you. My name is Maggie. Welcome to Granger."

"I suppose in a town this size, everyone knows everybody."

Maggie nodded. "You're absolutely right, honey. We can spot an outsider as soon as they step across the city limits. If you don't

25

mind my asking, what brings you to Granger?"

"A few months ago, I came across an article on the town and decided it would be the perfect place to visit," Lydia stated. "I've always wanted to see Montana."

"Since Laney Broward won a gold medal at the Olympics, we have had a flood of folks from all over. Some come to visit and end up staying. I think it's wonderful. This town can use some new blood, if you ask me." Maggie took her by the arm. "C'mon over here, honey. Let me introduce you around. Maybe that way the folks will stop staring you down. We're a curious bunch here in Granger."

Lydia chuckled.

They moved about the room, pausing here and there so that Maggie could introduce her.

"I don't think I've ever met people who were so warm and welcoming," Lydia said.

Maggie led the way to where a group of important-looking attendees were standing. Lydia glanced over her shoulder, searching for Wesley. She found him standing near the buffet table with two other men.

Their gazes met and locked.

After what seemed like an eternity, Lydia turned her attention back to Maggie.

"Where are you from?"

"Los Angeles," Lydia replied. She stole a glance to where she last saw Wesley. Lydia's eyes traveled the room, searching when he was no longer there. She found him sitting down at a table with his sister. The two appeared deep in conversation.

At the sound of her name, Lydia pasted on a smile as Maggie continued to make introductions.

As they neared the table where the Broward family was sitting, Lydia released a soft sigh. It seemed the men had decided to leave the table for whatever reason.

"Hey, y'all," Maggie uttered in greeting. "I want to introduce you to Lydia. She's visiting our lil' town."

Gwendolyn smiled. "It's very nice to meet you, dear."

"It's a pleasure to meet you, as well," Lydia responded. She turned her attention to Laney and said, "Congratulations on winning the gold."

"Thank you," Laney murmured. "I hope you'll enjoy Granger."

"I'm sure I will. It's so beautiful here."

Lydia was glad when they moved on to the next table. Maggie was intent on her meeting everyone at the fundraiser, it seemed.

"Oh, the auction is about to start," Maggie said. "We should take our seats."

"Thanks for the introductions," Lydia told her. "I appreciate it."

"Happy to do it," Maggie responded with a smile. "I'll catch up with you after the auction."

Lydia walked quickly, her heels tapping a steady rhythm across the dance floor.

The moment she had been waiting for all night long had finally arrived.

Lydia was ready.

CHAPTER 2

"Get ready, ladies, to *bid* money to win a date with some of our most eligible *males* in Granger. Winners get a romantic date featuring a delicious candlelight dinner, wine and dancing," the auctioneer announced.

Lydia felt a shiver of anticipation course down her spine. Single women all around the room rose to their feet and gathered near the stage. She was careful to remain near the back of the gathering group, farthest from the front.

"Let's start the bid at one thousand dollars for this handsome cowboy here," said the auctioneer. "Jameson Broward loves to travel and is looking to take one lucky girl on a romantic date exploring international cuisine. I don't know about you, but I love to eat, so this sounds like heaven."

Laughter and chuckles rang out across the room.

Lydia noted that Jameson wore a handsome smile, but that smile did not reach his eyes. He did not appear at all happy to be on the auction block.

She took a sip of her white wine. This was about to get interesting.

"One thousand dollars," a woman called out.

"Eleven hundred," a second woman countered.

"Fifteen hundred," another bid.

A young woman standing near Lydia won Jameson for five thousand dollars.

The Broward patriarch, Charles, also ignited a bidding war — between a twenty-something-year-old and a more mature woman, which Lydia found amusing.

The young woman's tenacity and wallet won out at three thousand dollars.

"Looks like Miss Patti Wier has won herself a cowboy and a gentleman," the auctioneer said.

Laughter and cheers rang around the room.

Now it was time for Wesley to step up on the auction block. Lydia knew instinctively that he would bring in the most money, and she was prepared.

"This handsome cowboy has a surprise in store for some lucky woman. Girls, I tried to pry the details out of him, but Wesley Broward's not telling. Don't you just love a man who can keep a secret?"

"One thousand dollars," Lydia heard someone yell out.

"Two thousand," another said.

She glanced around the room as others quickly tossed out bids.

The bidding was fast-paced and frenzied.

When the amount rose to six thousand dollars, only two women were still in a bidding war.

"Six thousand five hundred."

"Seven thousand dollars."

The room grew quiet.

It's time, Lydia decided.

"Ten thousand dollars," she said loudly.

The room was suddenly filled with tense silence as all eyes turned toward the young woman who had placed the highest bid in the charity event's history.

Amused, Wesley joined the others in the search. He usually brought in the most money, but this was a completely unexpected turn of events. Historically, the bids were never higher than six thousand dollars.

He continued to gaze around the room, searching for the woman who had just outbid the others. As the sea of people parted, he glimpsed a beauty wearing a stunning teal and purple gown. He had noticed her earlier. It had been a few fleeting glances at best, but they were enough to ignite his interest. She was not familiar to him, as he knew most of the women in Granger. However, the stranger seemed to know Maggie Dillon.

Maggie was married to the owner of the Double D Ranch. The redhead with big blue eyes was nice enough, but she loved to talk.

The stunning woman made her way gracefully toward the stage as the room erupted into loud clapping. Slowly and seductively, Wesley's gaze slid downward, giving her body a raking once-over.

"Do you know her?" Jameson asked his brother in a low voice.

"No, but I saw her for a split second with Maggie earlier." He didn't add that she had captured his interest and learning more about her was already on his agenda.

Wesley's breath caught in his throat as she neared the stage. She was gorgeous, and definitely not from around these parts. He was thrilled to be won by an outsider — and a beautiful one at that.

"Come on up, honey," the auctioneer said. "We want to get some pictures of our bachelors and their dates."

From his vantage point onstage, Wesley estimated her age to be in her middle to late twenties. He decided she was about five feet seven inches tall. She had a slender but curvy build. As she neared the stage, Wesley glimpsed her big brown eyes with long lashes, warm cocoa complexion and dark, curly tresses. He found himself looking forward to his date with this stranger.

Lydia blew out a breath as her stomach began to twist and ripple with nerves that had been shivering through her all evening. Those feelings intensified just as she was about to join Wesley on the stage.

Something vaguely sensuous passed between them.

"Hello, darlin'," he greeted in a low voice. "It appears you and I are going on a dream date."

Looking up into Wesley's handsome face, she smiled. "Yes, it does appear that way."

"Come closer," he whispered. "I won't bite."

The underlying sensuality of his words captivated Lydia. She could clearly tell that he was a man who enjoyed the attention of women.

Wesley wrapped an arm around her and

held her snugly as they posed for pictures before leaving the stage.

Lydia relaxed, sinking into his cushioning embrace. Her skin tingled where Wesley touched her, his nearness making her senses spin.

"What is your name, pretty lady?" he asked while walking her back to her table.

"Lydia LaSalle," she responded with a smile. "And I already know that you are Wesley Broward. It's nice to finally meet the man I've heard so much about."

Lydia could tell from the look of surprise on his face that she had caught him momentarily off guard, but he seemed to recover quickly.

"I hope everything you've heard presents me in a positive light."

"It does," she confirmed.

"You have me at a disadvantage, I'm afraid," Wesley stated. "What brings you to Granger?"

"I heard it was a lovely place to visit," Lydia responded smoothly. "I thought I'd come see for myself, and it really is beautiful. It's definitely one of Montana's hidden gems."

"How long are you staying in town?"

"I'm not sure," she answered. "For a few weeks at least."

Wesley seemed to be peering at her intently, and Lydia was strangely flattered by his interest.

"How does Saturday night work for you?" he inquired. "For our date."

She nodded. "I don't have any pressing plans, so it's perfect."

He sat down on the vacant chair beside her, and once again, when his gaze met hers, her heart turned over in response.

This is so crazy, Lydia thought to herself. *The man is just being nice to me. I just paid ten thousand dollars for a date with him. I would be nice to anyone who paid that much money to go out with me.*

All eyes seemed to be on the two of them, but Wesley didn't seem to mind. He continued to gaze at Lydia, almost as if he were photographing her with his eyes.

"You're staring at me," she murmured.

"I can't help myself," Wesley said matter-of-factly. "You are beyond beautiful."

She laughed. "This is the first time I've been told that. I heard that cowboys have a way with the ladies. I'm beginning to believe it."

Lydia tried to throttle the dizzying current racing through her. She wanted to resist his charm, but she could not. She was powerless to resist.

"Would you like to dance?" Wesley asked, gesturing toward the dance floor.

"Sure," Lydia replied with complacent buoyancy.

She rose to her feet in one fluid motion, prompting him to follow suit.

On the dance floor, Maggie brushed past her, gave a thumbs-up and winked.

Lydia swayed to the music.

"You're a good dancer," Wesley told her.

"So are you," Lydia responded.

"Do you do any line dancing?" he asked.

Lydia shook her head. "I'm willing to learn," she responded with a grin.

The next song that came on provided Wesley an opportunity to give her some instruction.

"You're a quick learner," Wesley said as they left the dance floor.

She laughed. "I don't know about that. I was awful out there."

This time he did not take a seat when they returned to her table. Instead, he picked up her right hand and kissed it. "It's been a pleasure talking to you," Wesley said. "My mother's over there glaring at me, so I need to make my rounds. My work is never done, it seems."

"I understand," she responded. His family was a major sponsor, so this was a working event for Wesley. "It was nice to meet you."

"I will see you Saturday."

Lydia nodded. "It's a date."

Lydia hummed softly as she sat down on the edge of her bed and removed her silver high-heeled sandals. She rose to her feet and slipped off her gown, replacing it with a pair of knit shorts and a tank top.

She strolled into the bathroom to remove her makeup and brush her teeth before settling down in the middle of the bed with her cell phone.

"Hey, it's me," Lydia said. "I have some really good news to report. Everything went according to plan. Wesley and I have a date on Saturday."

"That's wonderful."

Smiling, she responded, "I knew you'd be pleased."

"So tell me, Lydia . . . is Wesley Broward really as handsome in person as he is in all the magazines?"

"He is," Lydia confirmed. "One thing's for sure — he definitely seems to have a high regard for himself."

There was a chuckle on the other end of the line. "I'm sure he's very charming."

Lydia settled back against a stack of pillows. "He was nice enough, but I didn't get to spend much time with him."

"Why not? Lydia, that's why I sent you to Montana. What were you doing all night?"

"I couldn't exactly monopolize his time," Lydia stated. "He and his family cosponsored the fundraiser, so he was busy much of the night. I did exactly what you wanted. I won Wesley at the auction and we are going to have dinner together this weekend." She paused a moment before adding, "Besides, if I'd come on too strong, that would've made him suspicious."

"I suppose you're right. Just make sure you find out everything there is to know about Wesley Broward and his family. Speaking of which, did you get to meet his family?"

"Briefly," Lydia responded.

"What were they like?"

"They seemed nice enough," she said, wondering yet again why her boss seemed so interested in the Broward family. "What is this really about?"

"I pay you enough to not ask questions, Lydia. *Just do your job.*"

Her employer disconnected the call before she could utter a response.

She released a sigh of frustration. There were times when Lydia wondered why she ever agreed to work for someone so self-absorbed and demanding, but it was a prime opportunity. Lydia had dreams of getting into entertainment management, and her job could provide her a foot in the door.

Her employer could be so sweet when she wanted to be, but then she could also be hard as nails, which probably served her well in her profession.

The one question that remained in Lydia's mind was regarding her employer's connection to Wesley. It was pretty obvious that the two did not know each other.

What's really going on?

Lydia knew she would remain in the dark until her boss decided to open up about her plans concerning Wesley.

Thinking about him prompted the beginnings of a smile. Lydia found herself to be quite taken by his cowboy "Code of the West" charm. Her body tingled at the thought of seeing him on Saturday for their date. The memory of why she had come to Granger invaded her thoughts. She liked Wesley, but not only that, she just wasn't comfortable with her role in this scheme. It bothered her that her employer was acting so suspiciously. Lydia vowed that she would not do anything that would hurt Wesley.

She thought about the way he gazed at

39

her upon her approach to the stage earlier. Lydia had not missed his obvious examination and approval. However, Lydia had not expected to be so drawn to Wesley. She had to find a way to maintain control over the situation.

Sighing softly, Lydia settled into her bed. It had been an exciting evening, but she was tired.

Tomorrow she'd be busy putting her employer's plan into action.

CHAPTER 3

Wesley had to be up early the next morning, so he left shortly after eleven o'clock to return to the ranch. He'd agreed to drive his grandfather home on the way, since his parents and siblings were still at the hotel.

"That was a purdy lil' woman that wrangled you tonight, Wes," his grandfather said as he removed his tuxedo jacket. "Right purdy girl."

He chuckled. "From the looks of it, you didn't do too bad yourself, Grandpa."

"I just have to remember to have her home before her curfew."

Wesley threw back his head and laughed. "I noticed some of the women weren't happy at being outbid by a twenty-year-old — especially Eugenia Maple. She's had her eye on you since her husband died last year."

"She may have her eye on me, but I'm not interested," Charles uttered. "I know for a fact she drove Henry to his grave.

From what he used to tell me, Eugenia is not an easy woman to live with. I'll tell you this, Wes. That's not how I intend to live out the rest of my days — with a nagging woman."

"I want someone I can be friends with," Wesley stated. An image of Lydia materialized in his mind.

"Friends with," his grandfather repeated.

He nodded. "I want a woman I *like* being around and want to spend time with. I want a woman I can talk to about anything and she's actually interested in hearing what I have to say. I want a woman who will be honest and trustworthy. Someone who won't play games."

"Your grandmother was . . . She was a good woman. Outspoken and told the truth, even when you didn't want to hear it. Lawd knows . . . I miss that woman."

"Grandpa, I miss her, too," Wesley confessed. "Things aren't the same without her."

He headed to the front door. "Don't forget to take your medicine, Grandpa."

Charles waved his hand in a dismissive gesture. "Good night, Wes."

Laughing, Wesley responded, "I'll see you in the morning." His grandfather resented being treated like an old man. He was independent and intent on doing things his own way.

Wesley drove from the main house to his own place, a three-bedroom cabin that had been renovated six years prior.

Inside, he walked straight to his bedroom and undressed.

As he prepared for bed, Wesley's thoughts turned back to Lydia. His attraction to her was instant, igniting an interest in learning more about her. The fact that she had her own money was also attractive to him. He had long grown tired of gold diggers.

Lydia was different from the women he was used to dealing with. Unlike in the past, Wesley found himself looking forward to Saturday night.

Maybe it was because she wasn't from Granger. Whatever the reason, his interest in her was piqued. He was looking forward to getting to know Lydia better.

Wesley had no doubt in his mind that he would be seeing more of her after Saturday night. It was just the beginning for them.

Saturday arrived along with her long-anticipated date with Wesley. Lydia fingered her curls as she eyed her reflection in the mirror.

I feel like an excited schoolgirl experiencing

her first date. She giggled at the thought. It had been a long time since she'd felt this way. Lydia had to remind herself that this wasn't a real date.

The thought put a damper on her excitement. It was a ruse to get close to Wesley.

The ringing of her cell phone provided a wonderful distraction for her. Lydia picked it up, looking at the caller ID. "I can't talk to you right now," she whispered.

She tossed the cell on the bed and then turned her attention back to her appearance. Even though it was not a real date, Lydia wanted to look her best for Wesley. She had a feeling that it would be a night she would never forget. Wesley had been very secretive about their date and had given her no details. *I can't read too much into this,* Lydia reminded herself. The only reason he was taking her out was because she'd donated ten thousand dollars to charity. It wasn't even her own money that she'd used. She was not even being her true self.

A thread of guilt snaked down her spine. Lydia liked Wesley, and deep down it really bothered her that she was not being completely honest with him.

She kept trying to convince herself that it didn't matter. Lydia was in Granger to find out everything she could about Wesley, and

44

then she would be returning to Los Angeles.

Yet, she could not deny the spark of excitement at the prospect of spending time with Wesley Broward, even if it was a job.

A job, she acknowledged, she would find enjoyable.

Lydia jumped at the sound of a knock on the door.

She did a final check of her makeup and hair before opening the door.

Wesley raised an eyebrow a fraction at the sight of her.

Their gaze met and held.

Lydia could almost feel the movement of his breathing. "Hello," she whispered.

He wore a starched white shirt and a pair of black denim pants with highly polished cowboy boots. The sight of Wesley standing in her hotel room made Lydia's heart beat rapidly and her pulse quicken. A delicious shiver of wanting ran through her.

She could barely tear her gaze away from him.

Neither one said a word.

After a few moments, Lydia burst into a short, nervous laugh to break the silence. "I guess we should get a move on."

Wesley nodded. "Yes, ma'am, but there's one thing you need to do before we go."

Confused, she met his gaze. "What is it?"

"You need to take off that dress."

The heavy lashes that shadowed her cheeks flew up. "Excuse me?" *What's wrong with my dress?* she wondered.

Wesley eyed the silk dress Lydia was wearing and smiled. She looked exquisite — too exquisite for the evening he'd planned for them. His gaze traveled to her shoes. "You might want to wear something a little more comfortable," he told her.

She glanced down at her clothes and asked, "Why? Where are we going?"

"It's a surprise," he murmured.

"I'm sure I'll be fine," Lydia responded.

"Okay," he said. "Don't say I didn't warn you."

She was quiet on the drive to the surprise location. Wesley drove to the last place anyone would think he would bring a date.

When he pulled into the parking lot of their destination, he stole a peek at Lydia. Her expression was unreadable.

"What's the name of this place?" she asked.

"Shank of the Evening Saloon."

"That's quite an interesting name," Lydia responded as she eyed the wooden shack. To most outsiders, it probably looked like an old eyesore, but not to her. "How old is this place?"

"It's been around for almost seventy-five years," he told her. "And it's a favorite of ranchers in the area."

Wesley noticed that she looked mildly surprised that he would bring her to such a gritty establishment whose interior walls were covered with old license plates, news clippings and photos of the past.

But if Lydia was at all shocked by his choice of venue, she certainly hid it well.

Lydia had no idea that the only reason he'd brought her to this place was to gauge her reaction. Quite a few women were interested more in his money than in him. Wesley wanted to get a feel for Lydia. He was curious as to why she'd bid so much money for a date with him. It had to be to get his attention.

Lydia had no idea that she had already sparked Wesley's interest in her. He cleared his throat, pretending not to be affected.

"What would you like to drink?" he asked, fully expecting her to order some girlie drink.

She glanced around the saloon, and then said, "I'd like a beer."

Wesley was surprised. He also noted that she didn't flinch at the less-than-refined behavior of some of the patrons around

47

them, and he was impressed. There was more to this city girl than he first thought.

Their beers arrived.

Lydia took a sip of hers.

He smiled when she didn't make a face at the taste. This was a woman who truly seemed to enjoy a beer every now and then.

"You look surprised," she said. "You've never seen a girl drink beer?"

"I never thought a city girl like you would ever drink one, or be comfortable in a place like this."

"I'm an occasional drinker," Lydia told him. "I may drink a beer once or twice a year. My drink of choice is a chocolate raspberry martini, but I'm pretty sure I won't find that here."

Wesley chuckled. "You're right about that."

"As for this place, this is nothing new to me," Lydia stated. "I've been in places similar to this back home in New York."

She swayed to the music. "I've never been much of a country music lover, but it's actually growing on me."

"I like some of it," he responded. "I'm more of a jazz lover."

"Really?"

He nodded. "There's no better music than jazz. My favorites are the samba/bossa nova standards, especially if I want some soft, pleasant jazz to relax to."

"Wesley, what do you do for recreation?" Lydia asked. "Do you play any sports?"

"I played football and basketball in high school," he answered. "I didn't do much in college though because of a knee injury. I focused more on my studies. As for now, I enjoy riding my horse in the evenings — it relaxes me after a long day. I play basketball every now and then with some guys I went to college with. What about you? What do you do for fun?"

Lydia smiled at him. "Not much these days."

"Why is that?" Wesley asked.

"No special reason," she responded. "I guess I've been trying new things, such as coming to Montana." Lydia met his gaze. "I'm glad I did."

"I have to say that I'm glad you decided to visit our lil' town. I never would've met you otherwise."

"I have to say that I'm glad I decided to come to Granger. It's beautiful here."

She took a sip of her beer. "I'd really like to know more about you, Wesley. I've never met a man like you."

"Call me Wes. Wesley sounds so formal."

Lydia grinned. "Okay . . . Wes it is." She

paused a heartbeat before saying, "Tell me something about you that most people don't know."

Normally Wes would deflect this attempt at getting personal with some self-deprecating humor, but something about Lydia prompted him to answer honestly. "I want something more out of life. More than ranching."

His response was not what she would have expected him to say. "Then why don't you go after whatever it is that you want?" she asked. "Life is short. Live every moment as if it's your last."

Wesley met Lydia's gaze and smiled. "You're right." It just wasn't that easy for him, however. He had to think of his family and what his choices would mean for them.

He leaned forward and asked, "Would you like to dance?"

She surprised Wesley by removing her high-heeled sandals. "Sure."

He broke into a grin. "C'mon, darlin'."

Perspiration dotted her brow as they made their way off the dance floor. Lydia was having the time of her life. The establishment looked like nothing more than an old shack, but the music was great.

Fanning herself with her left hand, Lydia

said, "I need a glass of ice water."

"Have a seat and I'll get you some," Wesley told her.

She returned to their table and sat down.

A few minutes later, Wesley walked over with her water. "Here you are, darlin'."

"Thanks," Lydia murmured as she accepted the glass from him. "You are a life saver."

He dropped down into the seat beside her.

She turned to face Wesley and whispered, "This may surprise you, but I am having a great time."

He eyed her. "Really? In a place like this?"

"Yes," Lydia confirmed. "It doesn't look like much, but I like it."

"I have a confession to make," Wesley stated.

"What is it?"

"I brought you here to get some type of reaction from you. I wanted a glimpse into the real you."

"I guess you expected me to throw some type of tantrum." Wesley had no idea that a place like this was nothing new to Lydia. She used to frequent some of the hole-in-the-wall joints back in Syracuse when she was in college. While she had been surprised in his choice, she was not repulsed by the establishment.

"I didn't know what to expect, Lydia. I have another admission. From the moment I saw you at the gala, you've had my interest piqued."

Lydia's heart leaped at his words. It was at that moment that she realized just how much she wanted Wesley to find her desirable. Not just to play into her employer's plan, whatever it really was. But for her own satisfaction.

"Be honest," he said. "You're not a little bit shocked that I brought you to a place like this? I'm sure you expected to be taken to some expensive restaurant."

"I did," she confessed. "But it doesn't matter. Wesley, I'm not some snobby type, if that's what you were worried about. I'm just a normal flesh-and-blood woman."

"I'm glad to hear it," Wesley said with a smile. "Relieved actually."

Lydia laughed. "I have to confess that I wondered the same about you. I had hoped you weren't some stiff-shirt type of snob."

"I'm sure you know that's not me by now."

She nodded. Lydia thought she detected a flicker in his intense eyes. She shifted in her chair as she struggled to regain control of her emotions.

I'm here to do a job, she reminded herself.

Getting involved with Wesley would be a huge mistake. One she could not afford.

CHAPTER 4

Laughing, Wesley checked his watch. "Lydia, I'm so sorry. I made reservations for us at a restaurant in Helena and booked a helicopter to take us there, but we will never make it in time."

"I'm sure we can just grab something here in town," she responded. Lydia did not care much for helicopters, so she was perfectly fine with staying in Granger for dinner.

"I promised you an unforgettable evening, and I'm not about to welch out on a deal. Why don't you come out to the ranch? I'll have Rusty prepare a special meal for us."

"But what about your family?" she asked. "I don't want to intrude."

"Most likely, they have already eaten and will have retired for the evening."

"Wesley, you really don't have to go to all of this trouble. I'm having a great time with you. We can stay here as far as I'm concerned."

"I don't know about you, but I'm hungry."

"So am I," Lydia admitted. "Why don't we just go back to the hotel and have dinner?"

He shook his head no. "It's all settled. We are going to the ranch." His tone brooked no argument. "Just give me a few minutes to talk to Rusty."

Wesley made a quick phone call.

"Dinner will be ready by the time we arrive," Wesley announced as he put away his phone.

"Are you sure that we won't interrupt your family's evening?"

"We won't," he confirmed. "Rusty said that they are all in their rooms."

They walked outside to the car.

Wesley opened the door for Lydia and waited until she was safely inside before walking around to the driver's side.

"I promise you that you won't regret this," he told her. "Rusty is dynamic when it comes to preparing meals."

Lydia was enjoying her time spent with Wesley immensely. She didn't need a fancy restaurant or a meal prepared by an award-winning chef. She found that she did not want this night to end. Wesley was turning out to be so much more than she ever expected.

She reminded herself once more that she would have this night with him, but in a couple of weeks, she would be headed back to Los Angeles.

"Welcome to the BWB Ranch," Wesley said as he drove through the entrance.

Lydia was in awe at the sight of such opulence. She had seen photographs of the home and knew that the three-story wooden abode boasted five thousand square feet of living space and another five or six thousand square feet of covered porches. "What a beautiful house," she murmured.

"My parents designed every inch of it."

"I can't wait to see the interior." Lydia wanted a firsthand view of this luxurious home that had been featured in several magazines.

Although Wesley was not aware of it, Lydia had a copy of the Browards' floor plan.

The master bedroom loft touted two baths, something she had never heard of but thought it particularly useful.

Gwendolyn Webb Broward and her husband, Steven, met them in the foyer.

Lydia glanced over at Wesley, then back at his parents.

"I really hope we are not imposing," she

told them.

"You're not," Gwendolyn assured her. "My husband and I are retiring upstairs, so you and Wes have the house to yourselves. We just came down to get something to drink."

She and Wesley bade them good-night.

"I didn't expect to see them," Lydia whispered.

"Everything's fine. You can relax." He took her by the hand and said, "I'll give you a tour."

Lydia inhaled the sweet-smelling scent of the cedar wood as they went from room to room.

"Let me guess . . . this is where the men gather," she said when they entered a sports bar–inspired entertainment area with a wet bar bedecked in retro neon beer signs.

Wesley chuckled. "Yeah, this is the man cave."

They ended up in a great room with an extremely tall tongue-and-groove ceiling, wide-plank walnut floors and a larger-than-life fireplace.

They settled down on a leather couch.

"This ranch has been in your family for years," Lydia began. "Is the original homestead still on the property? I'm just curious."

57

"It is," Wesley confirmed. "It's where I live."

"I think you mentioned that your grand-father lives here, as well. I guess I thought that he resided in that home."

"He did," he responded. "Up until a few years ago. He's in his eighties and doesn't need to live alone, so my parents convinced him to move into the main house with them. My siblings also have their own places on the ranch. We have a dormlike facility where our workers live."

"This is all very impressive, Wes. I'd love to hear more about your family history." Lydia loved history. She had even done research on African-American cowboys before coming to Granger.

He rose to his feet. "I'll tell you while we eat dinner."

Lydia allowed him to help her up. She followed him into the massive dining room. There was enough room for twenty people to eat.

She and Wesley sat down at one end of the table where plates of food had been arranged for them, complete with candles and soft music.

After saying grace, Lydia sampled the deviled crabmeat in a mini bread bowl. "This is so delicious," she murmured.

"Rusty can whip up a five-star menu or supper for a bunch of hungry cowboys like it's nothing," Wesley stated.

She tried the pasta and caviar — a combination she would have never thought to put together but found delectable.

Picking up her napkin, she wiped her mouth. "Tell me about your family's rich history."

"The ranch was founded by my great-grandfather Silas in 1930. He and his wife, Olivia, had four sons, two of whom stayed in Granger and worked the ranch. One of those sons is my grandpa. In fact, the house my grandfather was born in still sits on the property. I live in that house. I remodeled it a few years ago, but I kept most of it the same as the original."

"How did your family get into breeding heritage farm animals?" Lydia inquired.

Wesley broke into a grin. "It was my dad's idea. Some folks thought this was just another crazy idea of his — he was always coming up with ideas about cattle breeding that seemed over the top. Folks used to tell my grandpa that his son was going to run the ranch into the ground, but turns out, my dad's idea was a good one."

"Now it's your turn," he said. "Tell me about your family."

"Well, my story is nothing like yours," Lydia responded, swallowing guilt over the lie she was about to tell. "My parents built a comfortable lifestyle by opening a couple of high-end boutiques."

"I'd say they are more than comfortable," he said. "Ten thousand dollars is a lot of money. No one in the history of that auction has ever bid that much money."

"It benefits those less fortunate," she replied. "I don't think you can put a price on helping others."

Wesley nodded in agreement.

Lydia wiped her mouth on the edge of her napkin. She prayed he wouldn't ask additional questions about her family because she did not want to lie to him any more than she already had.

"There's chocolate chip pie for dessert," Wesley announced.

The food was delicious, but Lydia found that she had lost her appetite. "Oh, wow . . . I'm afraid I don't have any room left. I'm stuffed."

"Would you like some coffee?"

"No thank you," she murmured. "I'm fine."

They finished up and returned to the great room.

Lydia heard footsteps and turned around.

"I didn't know anyone was down here," Jameson stated as his surprised gaze landed on her and stayed. "I thought tonight was your date night. Aren't you two supposed to be having dinner in Helena?"

"Yeah," Wesley responded. "But we ended up here instead."

"Whose idea was this?"

"Mine," Wesley responded.

"Wes, can I speak with you for a moment?" Jameson requested. His tone suggested that he would not take no for an answer.

"Sure." Wesley rose to his feet. "I'll be back shortly."

Although he retained an air of pleasantry, there was a distinct hardening of Jameson's gaze. From the expression on his face, Lydia could tell that he was not at all pleased to find her here at the ranch. She was irked by his cool, aloof manner.

She had no idea why a man who knew nothing about her showed such disdain toward her. Lydia tried not to let it bother her, but deep down Jameson's obvious dislike where she was concerned was a bit unsettling.

It was best to stay as far away from Jameson as possible. He did not trust her, and Lydia felt the same way about him.

■ ■ ■ ■

"Why did you bring her here?" Jameson questioned when they entered the library.

A shadow of annoyance hovered in his eyes. "Wes, she won you at an auction. You could have just taken the woman to an expensive restaurant for dinner and sent her on her way after paying the check. What in the world are you doing?"

Wes gave a slight shrug. "I like her."

"This date is nothing more than a fundraiser," Jameson stated. "Remember that."

"Why are you always so negative?" Wesley ripped out the words impatiently. "Not every woman in this world has a hidden agenda."

"How can you be sure that Lydia doesn't have one?"

"What would she be after, Jameson?" Wesley asked. "She clearly has money of her own. You were there. You heard how much she bid at the auction."

"What do you really know about her? Why is she here in Granger?"

"Lydia's on vacation."

Jameson laughed. "You can't be serious. She just decided to come to Granger for vacation and partake in our charity auction.

Wes, don't you find it strange that she bid so much money on you? Ten thousand dollars on a man she's never met before. Trust me, there's more to the story, and I would advise you to find out what's really going on before getting involved with her."

"Involved . . . I just met the woman, Jameson. What are you talking about?"

"I have a feeling that she was targeting you in particular."

"I don't believe that," Wesley uttered.

"Just heed this warning. I would be very careful if I were you, Wes."

"You don't have to worry, big brother," Wesley reassured him. "I have everything under control. Lydia LaSalle is a woman I'm interested in getting to know better, but this doesn't mean that I'm looking to rush into a relationship with her. It's not like she's planning to live in Granger. She will be going back home to Los Angeles — we may never see each other again."

"Are you sure you're not just looking for a distraction from the real issue at hand?"

He glared at Jameson, frowning. "What are you talking about?"

"Have you decided yet what you want to be when you grow up?" his brother asked.

"What do you mean by that?"

"I think you know the answer to that question."

"I need to get back to my date," Wesley stated. "I'll see you in the morning."

Wesley experienced a gamut of perplexing emotions, but he refused to let them ruin his evening with Lydia. He understood his brother's concerns when it came to women, but Wesley wasn't worried about Lydia.

She was a different type of woman than what he usually encountered.

He paused in the doorway, observing as Lydia channel-surfed. She paused on the Discovery Channel. Wesley bit back a smile as she settled back to watch a documentary on chimpanzees.

She has a thing for monkeys, he thought.

Amused, he joined her on the sofa.

Lydia glanced at him. "Is everything okay with your brother?"

Wesley nodded. "Jameson can be very intense at times, but he's harmless."

"I get the feeling that he doesn't care much for me."

"He doesn't know you," Wesley responded.

"You really don't know anything about me, either," she pointed out.

"You're right, so why don't you tell me about yourself?"

"We've just had a really nice dinner," Lydia responded. "I'd rather not bore you into falling asleep."

"There is something I really need to know. I know that you donated the money for charity, but why did you bid on me?" Wesley inquired of Lydia. "You and I had never met, so why did you do it?"

"I told you," she responded. "I'd heard some really nice things about you, and I came across a couple articles about you and your family a few months ago. I was impressed with what I read. One of the things I admire most is your community efforts."

"But why didn't you bid on my brother or my grandpa?"

Lydia shrugged. "I don't know . . . I guess I just liked you best of all."

Wesley grinned. "I'm a lucky man."

"I have to confess that I almost bid for your grandfather though. It was a very hard decision."

He chuckled. "This is not the first time I've been told that. I guess my grandpa is still a ladies' man. I have a confession to make, as well. I'm glad you chose me because I wanted to meet you. I don't know . . . I felt a special connection to you from the first moment I laid eyes on you. I saw you a couple of times at the fundraiser, but I didn't get a chance to meet you until the auction."

Lydia was equally drawn to her date, which only served to make her feel guilty. She was not being honest with Wesley, and it bothered her. Lydia wanted him to know the real her — not some character she had created.

"I'm so sorry, Wes," she told him abruptly. "I didn't realize the time. I should head back to the hotel."

"Why don't you stay here at the ranch?" he suggested. "I'll take you back in the morning."

Shaking her head no, Lydia responded, "I don't want to impose on your family like this." She needed to leave before she spilled out the truth.

"They won't mind," Wesley assured her. "We have plenty of room. Lydia, you're more than welcome to stay at my place, but I don't want you to get the wrong idea."

"I really think that it's best that I go back to the hotel." She gazed at him. "I can call for a car if you're not up to driving me back to Granger."

"Nonsense," Wesley uttered. "I'll drive you back."

"This has been a wonderful evening,"

Lydia told him once they were back at the hotel. "In all honesty, it is the best date I've had. I really hope that doesn't make me sound pathetic."

Wesley grinned. "It doesn't. I would classify this as my best date, too."

"I guess we both need to get out more."

He laughed.

Wesley escorted her up to her room. "I'd like to see you again."

CHAPTER 5

"I'm asking you out on a second date," Wesley stated when no response was forthcoming. He tried to gauge her reaction but could not.

"Wesley, you don't have to do this," Lydia replied a few moments later. "I had a lovely time with you, but I don't want you feeling obligated to ask me out a second time because we didn't have dinner in Helena."

"That's not it at all," he responded. "I never do anything I don't want to do. What I want is to take you out on a real date. We can see a movie or a play. There's a new Broadway show in Helena that I'd like to see."

"Why don't you give me a call tomorrow?" she said. "We can discuss it then."

Wesley surprised her by placing his lips to hers like a soft whisper. The kiss was slow and gentle.

"I've wanted to do that all night," he said

in a low voice.

Lydia looked up at him. "Good night, Wesley."

He smiled. "Sleep well."

She unlocked her door and stepped inside.

Lydia navigated over to the sofa and sat down. Even in remembrance, she felt the intimacy of his kiss, which sent the pit of her stomach into a wild swirl.

She liked Wesley Broward. Really liked him.

I don't think I can do this anymore, she thought. *I can't keep lying to him. It's not right.*

Lydia opened up her laptop, which she left on the coffee table earlier. The time on it read twelve forty-five, but she wasn't sleepy.

For the next thirty minutes, Lydia drank hot tea and read news articles on the internet.

Her nerves were already in shreds without adding caffeine to the mix, but there was nothing else available outside of soda.

She had to pull herself together. Lydia did not have time to waste twiddling her thumbs. Instead she had to come up with a solution she could live with. Especially if she wanted to pursue a job managing celebrities. She had to be a problem solver and be able to think quickly on her feet.

Maybe she was overthinking the situation, Lydia decided. Once she spoke with her employer, she might find herself on the next plane headed back to Los Angeles. Lydia had done as requested, so there was no other reason to keep her in Granger.

She would really miss Wesley, Lydia thought sadly. It would not be easy to leave him behind.

Ten voice mails.

The next morning, Lydia released a soft sigh as she stared down at her iPhone. She didn't bother to listen to her messages because they were all from her boss, and Lydia knew exactly what she wanted.

She climbed out of bed and padded barefoot into the bathroom.

Fifteen minutes later, a freshly showered Lydia dropped down on the left side of her bed. Sighing softly, she grabbed her phone off the nightstand. It was time to call her employer.

"Samara, it's me."

"I've been waiting around for your call." She sounded irritated. "I'm meeting my agent for breakfast, so we need to make this quick. How did your date with Wesley go?"

"Fine," Lydia responded.

"What did you find out?" Samara questioned, getting right to the point.

"Mainly the same stuff that we already knew about," Lydia answered.

She heard Samara heave a sigh of frustration and said, "I'm afraid I don't understand what you're looking for. Wes and his family are on the level, if that's what you are concerned about. They are very involved with their community and they are a close-knit family."

"So you're telling me that you didn't learn anything more about Wesley Broward, other than what we have already learned?"

"That's pretty much it," Lydia responded.

She was not willing to share any more of the conversation she had with Wesley. Although Lydia was not sure why, she felt protective of him. "When do you want me to come home?"

"I think you should stick around a little while longer," Samara told her. "Use this time to get to know the Browards better."

"Why are you so interested in Wesley and his family?"

Samara laughed. "You really read too much drama into everything, Lydia. If you must know . . . I've been offered a role in a Western and I wanted some research to make my portrayal more authentic."

"So why didn't you come to Granger

yourself?" Lydia inquired. "And why are you specifically focusing on Wesley?"

"I chose Wesley Broward because he seems very much like the hero in the movie. I'd read about his family during the Olympics. Don't worry — I'll be coming to Granger in the near future. Until then, I need you to stay there and keep researching Wesley. Date him, do whatever it takes."

"I've told you everything about him."

"Start writing down everything that you learn — sometimes the tiniest details about a person are the most telling ones. Who knows . . . it might improve my performance."

Samara Lionne had both fame and beauty. As Samara did, Lydia intended to work her way up in the business. Samara also refused to speak about her past. She advised Lydia that it was best for her career to maintain an aura of elusiveness.

Although Samara was not an easy person to work for, Lydia reminded herself daily that this is what she had to do to lay down a foundation for her future. Samara's mood swings were legendary, and it was often rumored that her emotionality was what made her a dynamic actress.

Lydia wished she knew what Samara was really after. She did not believe that this was just about a movie role. She was thrilled over the idea of getting closer to the cowboy, but she detested having to continue her ruse.

Nothing good could come out of a relationship based on deceit.

When Lydia opened her door that morning, she was greeted by a young woman holding a dozen pale pink roses.

"Miss LaSalle, these were just delivered here for you."

She took them from the woman. "Thank you. Just let me put these down and I'll get my purse."

"The tip was included, Miss LaSalle."

Her brows rose in surprise. "Oh, well, thanks again."

The young woman smiled. "It's my pleasure."

Lydia closed the door and held the flowers to her nose, inhaling their sweet fragrance. She carried them over to the coffee table and set them down.

She plucked the envelope from the roses, but before she could open it, there was another knock on her door.

Lydia got up and crossed the room quickly to open the door.

"Wes," she exclaimed in intense pleasure.

"What are you doing here?" She stole a peek over her shoulder, and then turned back to look at him. "The flowers are from you, right?"

"Yeah, the flowers came from me," he answered. "The reason I came by this morning is because I'm not good at waiting for some things. After last night, I wasn't really sure where things stood between us. I didn't know if I'd ever see you again."

"I thought that I would have to leave sooner than originally planned, but as it turns out, I will be staying in Granger a little while longer."

Wesley grinned. "I'm glad to hear it."

"I must look a mess," she muttered, running her fingers through her hair.

"No, you don't," Wesley quickly interjected. "You are naturally beautiful, Lydia. You don't need a bunch of cosmetics."

She gestured for him to have a seat on the sofa.

"How did you know that I love roses?" Lydia questioned as she sat down beside him.

"The perfume you wore last night was a light floral scent, so I just took a wild guess," Wesley responded.

His response triggered a smile on her face.

"I meant what I told you last night, Lydia.

I would like to spend more time with you."

Lydia wanted to spend time with him, as well — not just because Samara ordered her to do so. Wesley was a nice guy and he deserved the truth. The thought tore at her insides.

He surveyed her face for a moment. "What's wrong? You know, I should've asked if you're seeing someone."

"No, I'm not," Lydia responded. "I'm single."

"You look like something's bothering you."

"It is," she confirmed. Lydia sat in the chair, her slender fingers tensed in her lap. "Wes, I really like you and, well . . . I haven't been completely honest with you. I need to tell you the truth."

"I'd appreciate that," he said quietly. Something was flickering far back in his eyes. Disappointment?

Awkwardly, she cleared her throat. "First off, my name is Lydia Emerson. Despite how things may look, I am not an heiress. I work as a personal assistant for a well-known actress, and I'm here researching cowboys for an upcoming role."

"I really don't like being lied to," Wesley stated.

"I don't like lying," Lydia responded,

flinching at the tone of his voice. "This is why I'm telling you the truth now."

Wesley hesitated, measuring her for a moment. "Who is this actress?"

Lydia chose her words carefully. "Wes, I can't tell you that. I've already put my job on the line by telling you as much as I have."

"The money you bid . . . it was her money? So, you were faking all of this time to get close to me?"

"No, I wasn't faking anything," she answered thickly. "Yeah, the money was hers . . . but Wes, I really like you — there is nothing phony about my feelings."

He moved closer, gazing into Lydia's eyes as if trying to judge the truthfulness of her confession.

"I feel horrible for lying to you," she whispered.

Lydia realized that she was shaking, but it was not from fear. She knew deep down that Wesley would never hurt her, but he was disappointed in her.

She looked up at him with an effort. "I'm sorry, Wes."

Wes kissed her.

When he finally pulled away, he said, "If your boss wants information, we'll give it to her. I'll tell you anything you want to know as long as it's about being a cowboy or a rancher."

Lydia wasn't sure if he was joking or not. "Are you serious?"

Wesley nodded. "Yeah. If you want information about ranching, I'll give you a firsthand view."

Uncertainty crept into her expression. Although he seemed fine, Lydia wasn't sure things would ever be the same between them.

Wesley believed Lydia because he wanted to believe that his instincts were right about her.

He appreciated and admired Lydia for confessing the truth to him. Initially, he was disappointed to find that she had been lying about her identity, but Wesley understood the need for secrecy somewhat. He was curious about the actress she worked for, but he respected Lydia's wishes to withhold the woman's identity.

"Please say something," she whispered. "I want to know that we can get past this."

He glanced over at her and smiled. "We already have, sweetheart."

Lydia shook her head regretfully.

Wesley awarded her a smile. "I understand why you did it."

"I want you to know that you can trust

77

me, Wes. I . . ."

He reached over and took her hand in his own. "We're okay."

"Have you had breakfast?" Lydia inquired.

"No," he responded. "Why?"

"Would you join me in the restaurant downstairs? I'm starving." Lydia rose to her feet. "Oh, and I'm buying."

"You don't have to do that."

"I want to," she insisted with a smile. "I'm not taking no for an answer, Wes."

They left the suite and walked the short distance to the elevator.

"You're a very special woman, Lydia."

"Don't do that," she said. "Wes, please don't go putting me on a pedestal. You'll only be disappointed if I can't live up to it."

Wesley nodded in understanding as they stepped onto the elevator.

Lydia was correct in her assumptions. Many of the women in his past accused him of lacking the patience for human fallacy. He never considered that they just might be right. It was true that he held himself in high regard and he had high expectations of those he cared about.

Nobody's perfect, he reminded himself. *Not even me.*

A few minutes later, they stepped off the elevator and entered the restaurant.

They were seated quickly.

"What are your plans for today?" he asked her.

"I have some paperwork I need to complete and send off before noon," Lydia said. "Then I have a conference call scheduled at two."

"Sounds like you have a very busy day ahead of you."

She picked up the menu. "I do. That's one thing about this job — I do stay busy."

"Do you think you'll be up to spending some time with me later this evening?" Wesley inquired. "I was thinking that maybe we could see a movie and have dinner afterward."

"I'd really like that," Lydia stated.

The waitress arrived with two glasses of ice water, which she set down in front of them.

"Would you like anything else to drink besides water?" she asked.

"I don't need anything else," Lydia responded.

"I'd like a cup of coffee black." Wesley glanced over at her. "Are you ready to order?"

Lydia nodded.

The woman took their breakfast orders.

"Wes, are we really okay?" she inquired

after the waitress walked away. "I don't want you to think that I was playing some cruel joke on you, because I wasn't. It was nothing like that."

The sound of her voice affected Wesley deeply. He found it soothing and comforting. He deliberately shut off any awareness of the other people in the restaurant. "Sweetheart, I believe you and I want you to believe me now. We are fine. My opinion hasn't changed about you."

Lydia seemed to relax then.

"What type of role are you researching?" he asked. "Is it a rancher or something else?"

She nodded. "A female rancher and her family. They're a very close family — very similar to yours, I would say."

"You might get a better feel if you talk to the women in my family. Laney or my mother can actually discuss it from a woman's perspective," Wesley stated. "You should also talk to them." He was willing to do whatever he could to help Lydia with her task. He harbored a selfish reason, as well. It would give him an opportunity to get to know her better.

"That would be great," she murmured. "Do you think they'd mind talking to me?"

Wesley shook his head no. "My mother

80

would love it for sure. Laney won't mind, either."

"Would you ask them and let me know if it's okay?"

The food arrived.

Wesley gave the blessing.

He and Lydia both instinctively reached for the bottle of hot sauce.

"You like hot sauce on your scrambled eggs?" she asked him.

Nodding, Wesley responded, "You, too?"

They laughed.

"I knew we had something in common," he said. "Never thought it would be this."

Lydia sprinkled drops of hot sauce on her eggs. "How do you like your pizza?"

"With lots of meat and jalapeños."

Her eyes smoldered with fire as she met his gaze.

For a moment, neither of them spoke.

She broke the silence by clearing her throat softly. "Pizza . . . I like mine loaded with meat, as well, but with red pepper sprinkled on it. That's another thing we have in common."

"We're on a roll," he commented.

"I bet you like taking long walks," Lydia guessed aloud.

"How did you know that?"

"You live on a large ranch. You have to

love taking walks to get around on that property."

He chuckled.

"So am I right?" she asked. Lydia stuck a forkful of eggs in her mouth.

Wesley nodded. "I still enjoy taking a walk and enjoying the fresh air."

His gaze traveled slowly over Lydia's face, his pulse quickening at the speculation. His fingers ached to reach over and touch her. He made no attempt to hide the fact that he was watching her.

"You do that a lot, you know."

"Do what?" he asked.

"Stare at me like that," Lydia responded.

"It's because I find you incredibly attractive and very sexy. I could look at you for a thousand years and it would never be enough."

She fanned her hand back and forth. "If I didn't know better, I would say that you're trying to make me swoon."

Wesley threw back his head and laughed. "I don't think I've ever been told that."

"Are the rumors about you being a ladies' man true?" Lydia inquired.

"There was a time when it was true, but not anymore."

"What happened to change it?"

"I decided I wanted to find someone to

share my life with and so I needed to change me."

"That's very mature."

Wesley smiled. "A good woman wants a good man."

Lydia nodded in agreement. "True."

He picked up his water glass and took a long sip.

"I want you to know that I find you a very interesting man, Wes."

"Hopefully, your interest will keep you in Granger for a while," he responded. "I have to admit that I'm not looking forward to the day when you tell me you're leaving."

"I'm not looking forward to that day, either," Lydia confessed.

CHAPTER 6

Seated at the desk in her hotel suite, Lydia pulled her attention away from the laptop screen long enough to answer the telephone. "Hello."

"Hey, this is Maggie."

A smile spread across her face. "It's so nice to hear from you, Maggie. What are you up to?"

"Since you're new in town, I was thinking that I should take you to lunch. Are you free to join me this afternoon? There's a place in town called Las Margaritas, and it serves the best Mexican cuisine in the state of Montana. I remembered that you said it was a favorite of yours."

"My schedule's open," Lydia responded. Maggie had great timing. Wesley was working and she didn't relish eating alone.

"Good. Why don't we meet downstairs around noon?"

"I'll see you then," she told Maggie.

Lydia returned her attention to the project at hand: responding to media requests for interviews and appearances. Samara did not enjoy dealing with that aspect of her celebrity, so she expected Lydia to take care of it.

She put away her laptop shortly before she had to meet Maggie.

Lydia freshened up and then headed down to the lobby.

Maggie was dressed in a pair of skinny jeans, cowboy boots and a rhinestone-studded tunic.

"Don't you look charming?" she told Lydia. "I love that dress."

"Thanks," she responded. At the last minute, Lydia had decided to change into a black linen dress. She chose a pair of silver sandals to match her necklace and bangle bracelets.

The restaurant was two blocks away, so they walked from the hotel.

"Maggie, it was really sweet of you to invite me for lunch," Lydia stated once they were seated.

"I'm glad you accepted," Maggie responded with a smile. "I hate eating alone. I came to town to do some shopping, and when I was driving past this hotel, I thought about you."

Lydia picked up the menu.

"How are you enjoying our quaint little town?" Maggie asked after ordering two glasses of wine.

"I actually love it," Lydia responded. "I may do some sightseeing later this afternoon if I have time."

"If you have time?"

"I have some work to do," she explained.

Maggie looked puzzled. "I thought you were on vacation."

"It's more of a working vacation."

"Oh, that's no fun," Maggie uttered.

Lydia nodded in agreement.

Maggie leaned forward and said, "I have to tell you . . . you sure set tongues wagging at the auction. That was some bid for Granger's most eligible bachelor."

"It was all for charity," Lydia said.

"Uh-huh . . ." Maggie uttered before picking up her menu. "You know . . . I like you, Lydia. You have gumption. I have a feeling you and I are going to become great friends."

Lydia smiled in response. "I think so, too."

"So why did you really come to Granger?" Maggie asked. "Does it have something to do with Wes?"

"No," Lydia responded quickly. "Not really."

"C'mon, sugar, you can tell me," Maggie said with a grin.

Lydia decided to be honest. "I came here to do some research for the person I work for, Maggie. She's a high-profile actress, and she has an upcoming role in a Western."

"How exciting," Maggie exclaimed. "Is it someone I would know?"

"I'm sorry, but I can't tell you her identity," Lydia responded. "Not right now anyway."

"Well, poo . . ." Maggie huffed, sparking laughter from Lydia.

"Wesley is a good choice if you're looking to research a role. I can tell you that he's one of the best cowboys here in Granger. He really knows his stuff."

Lydia took a long sip from her glass of wine. "He came highly recommended."

"I'm sure he did."

She seized this opportunity to deflect the conversation. "Maggie, where are you from? I'm detecting a southern accent."

"I'm from Georgia. My husband, Dane, and I met when he was traveling with a rodeo. That man swept me right off my feet from the moment he jumped down off his horse and removed his hat. Girl, I was in love. Not that puppy-dog mess. I'm talking big-dog love."

Lydia chuckled.

"We got married three months later."

"Your husband's family owns the second-largest ranch in Granger, right?" Lydia asked.

Maggie nodded. "It's been in Dane's family for years. It hasn't been around quite as long as the BWB Ranch, but close." She shifted in her chair. "You obviously come from a privileged lifestyle. Tell me about yourself."

"There's really nothing to tell," Lydia stated. "I'm really not that interesting."

Maggie took a sip of her wine. "Humble as pie, I see."

Their food arrived.

Lydia felt as if she'd dodged a bullet just then. Thankfully Maggie didn't push for more information on her background while they ate. Her question had caught Lydia off guard, but it was a good thing. She had been truthful with Maggie. There really wasn't much to her life.

Lydia never discussed her childhood with any of her associates — only a few people in her inner circle knew the whole story. Many would be surprised to find that she grew up in a very poor household. Her father abandoned Lydia and her mother when she was just two years old. After that, she had only seen him maybe four or five times since then.

Lydia's life changed once she landed the job with Samara. This position afforded her entrance into the entertainment industry, thus opening the door wide enough to get her foot inside. Her ultimate goal was starting her own business in entertainment management.

Her job was demanding and Samara wore on her nerves at times, but her checks never bounced. Lydia had a strong work ethic, and she knew that jobs did not come easy. Besides, there were some perks to working with Samara. She never would've met Wesley if it had not been for the woman.

Lydia pushed away all thoughts of her leaving Granger and Wesley behind. She decided to enjoy every minute she had with him instead, however fleeting.

"I can't believe you didn't want to share your popcorn," Wesley said as they left the movie theater later that evening.

"You ate all of yours," Lydia countered with a short chuckle. "At the beginning of the movie. I wasn't going to let you eat mine."

"I see how you are."

"C'mon . . . don't be like that."

"I should be saying that to you," Wesley teased as he took her by the hand.

Lydia glanced upward at the moonlit sky. "It's a really beautiful night."

He agreed.

"This was a good night to walk to the theater," she stated. "If I lived in a town this size, I would walk everywhere."

Wesley wrapped his arm around her midriff. "Do you think that you could ever survive in a town like Granger?"

Lydia nodded. "I can live just about anywhere. I'm able to adapt to my surroundings."

"I see," he murmured.

"In a good way," she interjected.

When they arrived at the hotel, Lydia turned to him. "Would you like to come up?"

"Yes, ma'am."

They walked past the front desk.

"Did you see the way the desk clerk looked at us?" she asked in a low voice.

Wesley laughed. "She goes to our church. I believe I've just compromised your virtue."

Lydia met his gaze straight on. "Then I suppose you're going to have to marry me."

They laughed as they waited for the elevator.

Upstairs in her suite, Wesley pulled her

into his arms without preamble. First he kissed her forehead, then her eyes, and finally, he kissed her on the lips.

Lydia's lips were warm and sweet on his, causing his pleasure to radiate outward.

Wesley kissed her hungrily, as if each kiss was the last.

She locked herself into his embrace as he explored the hollows of her back. "I can't put into words just how much I want you," he whispered.

"I want you, too," she murmured. "But as much as I want to make love with you . . . Wes, we can't."

He pulled away from her slowly to look Lydia in the face. Wesley was fairly sure that he had not heard her correctly. "Why can't we?"

She took him by the hand and led him over to the sofa. "Wes, I have a rule when it comes to making love."

"Which is what?" Wesley inquired. He wasn't sure he really wanted to know. Women and their rules.

"I have always made it a habit not to rush into bed with anyone. I have to see where the relationship is going before I even consider intimacy. I hope that you can respect that."

"I can," he told her. "It's not what I

expected."

"You aren't too disappointed, are you?"

Deep down, Wesley did not like it, but he had no choice except to respect her decision. "I guess I'll take a cold shower to go."

"I'm sorry."

He smiled at her. "Don't apologize. It's fine."

"All I can say is that I'm worth waiting for, Wes."

"I certainly can't argue with that," he responded as he headed to the door.

She hugged him. "Thanks for understanding."

"It's good I have a thirty-minute ride to the ranch. Maybe by then my ardor will have cooled down."

Lydia held back a smile. She did not admit it to Wesley, but she was experiencing the same struggle. Her body was warm with her desire for him, but Lydia was determined to hold true to her word.

The next morning, Lydia was up bright and early.

She showered and dressed in a pair of designer jeans and a crisp linen blouse in a tangerine color. A pair of jeweled sandals matched the color of her top.

She ran her fingers through her curls,

fluffing them.

Lydia decided to do something for herself instead of staying cooped up in her room with the laptop. Before he left her room last night, Wesley mentioned that he had to travel to Helena with his brother and would be gone until tomorrow, so she was on her own.

She missed him, which came as a bit of a surprise although it shouldn't, Lydia reasoned. Her skin still tingled where Wesley had touched her. When she closed her eyes, she could feel his kisses as they burned a searing path to the pit of her stomach, igniting sparks of ecstasy. No man had ever had such a long-lasting effect on her.

Lydia reluctantly returned her attention to her work. She was not about to spend the rest of her day in this hotel suite. She wanted to see more of Granger.

Two hours later, Lydia strolled out of the hotel and climbed inside a rented automobile.

The crystal blue waters of the Fork River beckoned to Lydia as she was driving by, prompting her to park the car.

She resisted the urge to strip down to her underwear in a secluded area and take a swim beneath the big, aquamarine Montana sky. Lydia had happened upon this area nestled near what residents considered a popular fishing stream. She snapped a few pictures before returning to the rental car.

Lydia drove farther down the road where people longing for the daring side of life were kayaking, rafting or canoeing. She watched from the banks for a while.

Lydia reveled in the beauty of her surroundings.

She never considered living anywhere else outside Los Angeles, but now being in such a beautiful and tranquil place as Granger . . . *I could actually live here,* she silently acknowledged.

CHAPTER 7

The pale purple sky glowed on the eastern horizon and the stars still sparkled, although they were fading fast as night transformed to early dawn. Wesley sat atop his horse, stroking the animal gently.

"Today is a good day, Spartan," he murmured. After two days in Helena, Wesley was thrilled to be back at home, listening to meadowlarks as they sang from the sagebrush. From the cattails along the stream, red-winged blackbirds were starting their morning chorus. Just over the ridge, a pack of coyotes commenced their plaintive howling.

Beyond the road, Wesley observed a deer prancing about without a care in the world. It was a picturesque morning and one he suddenly had a desire to show Lydia. He knew instinctively that she would appreciate the beauty.

One of the qualities that attracted him to

Lydia was the freedom she exhibited. Wesley wondered what life must be like for her. He had never been the type of person who could just let go like that. Could she give up all that Los Angeles offered and live in a town like Granger?

It was too soon for him to have such dangerous thoughts. He cautioned himself to avoid getting carried away where his feelings were concerned.

Wesley forced himself to concentrate on his work. As much as he liked Lydia, he could not allow her to monopolize his thoughts. After all, he really did not know anything about her. She was not from Granger — a complete stranger, but one that he found intriguing.

"C'mon, Spartan," he said as he patted his horse. "Time for me to get back to work."

He caught up with Jameson. "Morning."

"I missed you at breakfast in the main house this morning."

"I got up and ate a bowl of cereal."

"Hey, did you hear about Grandpa's date last night?" his brother asked.

Wesley shook his head no. He had decided to have dinner at home alone last night after he and Jameson returned home from Helena.

"Turns out that Patti Weir had plans to set him up with her grandmother all along."

He burst into laughter. "Are you serious?"

Jameson nodded. "Yeah. Her grandmother was dressed and ready when Grandpa arrived."

"So what did Grandpa do?"

"He said they went out and had a nice dinner. Grandpa said he had a good time."

Wesley climbed off his horse. "This may turn out to be quite interesting."

Jameson followed suit. "That's what Grandpa said, as well. He didn't seem to mind the bait and switch."

"Dad's out here," Wesley announced. His father was over near the fence talking with two of the men who worked the ranch.

Wesley thought of his father as a strong self-starter whose vision for the family ranch had made them all very wealthy. His father knew ranching like the back of his own hand, and it was his life's work. He was a man more comfortable in a pair of faded jeans and cowboy boots than a suit. Wesley thought himself quite the opposite.

He was not afraid of the physical labor involved with ranching, but Wesley believed his strengths were more on the business side of things. He enjoyed purchasing land and smaller ranches. He had bought a property that was in shambles and renovated it into a working dude ranch. Wesley sold it for nearly three times what he paid for it.

"Why don't we go up to the office?" his father suggested when Wesley walked up. "There's a pile of new orders on the desk."

"I'll be there shortly," he responded. "I want to check out the regrowth on the north pasture. If it looks good, the cattle can be taken there to graze tomorrow."

"Okay. See you soon." Steven walked briskly toward his horse and climbed into the saddle.

He was in great physical shape for being in his sixties, Wesley acknowledged. He watched his father ride off before heading down to the north pasture.

Jameson had disappeared. No doubt he was checking on the Galloway cattle grazing on the south pasture.

I'll see him back at the office.

An image of Lydia formed in his mind, prompting a smile. Wesley wanted her so badly that his flesh seemed to burn for her body. It was as if she was his life source, and his soul hungered for her. He had never expected to feel such emotions where Lydia was concerned. Wesley had never been one willing to have a long-distance relationship, but he was not sure he could let her go so easily. He did not want her to go back to Los Angeles.

Memories of Wesley elicited a shiver of want in her. Lydia reminded herself that sex was not part of the equation — she was here to do a job. Still, Wesley was tall, gorgeous, with neatly cropped hair, brown eyes and a smile that seemed both sexy and charming at the same time.

The telephone rang, interrupting her thoughts.

Lydia dismissed the tantalizing images from her mind in favor of her reality — dealing with her boss. She answered her phone. "Hello."

"How are things going?"

"Great," Lydia responded. "Wesley has invited me to spend a day experiencing ranching from his perspective."

"That's a good sign. You two must be getting really close."

"I think he's just being nice." She decided it was best to keep her growing relationship with Wesley a secret from Samara. Lydia did not want to upset the temperamental actress unnecessarily.

Lydia picked up Wesley's photograph. "He's a nice guy."

Her words were met with cold silence.

"Samara," she prompted.

"The reason I called is because I'm in desperate need of a full-body massage," Samara blurted. "I need you to get me in to see Marlee today. After three, if possible. I want only Marlee to work on me. She's the best."

Lydia released a long sigh as she hung up her phone. Samara wanted her to court Wesley and stay on top of her spa treatments, as well. She wasn't about to let Lydia forget that she was nothing more than a lowly personal assistant to one of the top actresses in Hollywood.

Pushing the temperamental actress could lead to her being replaced in a heartbeat. There were days when Lydia questioned her career choice, but she was using this experience with Samara to land a job in entertainment management.

Despite her boss being a pain at times, Lydia was determined to make it in Los Angeles, if only to prove to her mother that she didn't make a mistake leaving home.

She picked up her planner, opening it up. A number of tasks were on her to-do list, including scheduling a spa appointment for Samara.

She picked up her cell phone and scanned through her address book.

"Samara Lionne would like to schedule a private session with Marlee," Lydia said when someone answered on the other end. "Anytime after three today."

As soon as she hung up, she sent Samara a text message confirming her appointment.

Lydia then went back over her calendar.

An hour later, she emailed her boss a full agenda for the rest of the week.

Samara was extremely high maintenance and relied heavily on Lydia to keep her abreast of her daily schedule.

After ensuring that Samara's needs were taken care of, Lydia decided to do some sightseeing. With any luck, she might run into Wesley again.

I won't get my hopes up.

Lydia walked out of the hotel and joined others on the sidewalk milling about downtown Granger, which was the epitome of diverse culture. Residents and visitors dressed in jeans and those in business suits moved along the busy streets. She truly appreciated the beauty of Granger. The town was warm, welcoming and filled with a unique community spirit.

One thing for sure, Samara could never survive in a place like this, which was probably the reason she sent Lydia to research this new role.

"There were some photographers hanging around near the entrance," Jameson uttered in frustration when he entered the main house, where the family had gathered for lunch. "I could hardly drive through the gate."

"Are they still there?" Wesley wanted to know. He was fine with newcomers in town, but he had a problem when it came to the invasion of his family's privacy. "I've already told them to stay off the property."

"Don't be so hard on them," his mother said. "Laney's success has certainly brought in a lot of publicity, but it's also increased sales for the ranch. This is a good thing."

"I get that," Jameson responded. "But I don't want people taking pictures of everything I do."

Wesley agreed.

"I can have my publicist request that they respect our privacy and stay away from the ranch unless invited," Laney stated.

Wesley eyed his sister. He was worried about her because Laney did not look well. He remained silent. She had been moody of late and he did not want to risk upsetting her. He had tried on several occasions to get Laney to open up, but she refused.

After Steven gave the blessing, Wesley reached for a sandwich and put it on his plate. "I don't know about y'all, but I'm starved. I worked up an appetite."

His father agreed. "I could eat a bear."

"I hear there's some actress looking to buy some property in these parts. She wants to buy a working ranch."

"Granger doesn't need a bunch of people moving here just because they have suddenly decided to be ranch owners," Jameson argued. "It would ruin everything the town represents."

"I don't agree," Wesley responded. "I think Granger can use some new blood. In fact, I've been entertaining offers for my parcels of land in Hastings."

"Are you crazy?"

He met his brother's angry gaze. "I'm not crazy, Jameson. I'm open to selling my property to the right person."

"I'm not sure I like this," his mother interjected. "There have been a lot of celebrities looking to purchase land here. I don't want to see Granger turn into a playground for the rich and famous."

"Mom, it's not what I want, either," Wesley expressed. "I'm not planning to sell to just anybody. It has to be the right person

— someone with a commitment to agriculture and land stewardship."

"How are things going between you and Wes?" Maggie asked when Lydia answered her phone.

She laughed. "Somehow I knew those were going to be the first words out of your mouth."

"Hey, it's all over town that you two have been seeing a lot of each other. So spill. . . ."

"I'm having a great time with Wesley. He is really a lot of fun and he's been a perfect gentleman."

"I'm not surprised," Maggie murmured. "Wes is one of the good guys."

Lydia agreed. "I think so, too."

"I keep forgetting to ask, but where did he take you for your dream date?"

"We went to the Shank of the Evening Saloon."

Maggie gasped in shock. *"He took you where?"*

"It was all in fun, Maggie," Lydia said with a laugh. "As it turned out, Wes and I had a great time there."

"Hey, I go to the Shank from time to time with Dane, but it's not what I'd consider the place for a first date."

"We had dinner reservations in Helena,

104

but we were having so much fun there that we never made it to the airport. He had rented a helicopter to take us to Helena." Lydia smiled. "It was still a nice evening though. Wes had his cook prepare a really nice meal for us at the main house."

"That Rusty is one of the best," Maggie stated. "I tried to steal him away from the Browards, but he wasn't interested in leaving. I even offered to double his salary. Thank God he didn't take me up on that offer. My Dane would have had me put down for sure. He's a wonderful man but cheap when it comes to stuff like that."

Lydia laughed. "Shame on you."

Shrugging, Maggie responded, "Hey, you can't blame a girl for trying to stay out of the kitchen."

"He is a genius when it comes to cooking," Lydia stated. "I was very impressed."

"Speaking of food, Dane and I are having a barbecue this weekend. If you're not busy, I'd really like for you to join us. We already sent out invitations to Wes and his family," Maggie stated. "I probably should've kept my big mouth shut, because I'm sure Wes will ask you to be his date."

"It's okay if he doesn't," Lydia said. "I have a personal invite from the hostess."

"You sure do, honey."

"What should I wear?" she asked, turning the subject of the conversation to fashion.

"Cute and sexy," Maggie responded. "I'ma tell you right now, there are some women who have been trying to get Wes's attention. Some of them will be at the barbecue, so you better come prepared, sugar. Girls don't always play nice, you know."

Lydia gave a short laugh. "Thanks for the heads-up, but I look at it this way, Maggie. If Wes is that easily distracted, then he's definitely not the man for me anyway."

"I knew I liked you."

She hung up from Maggie when Lydia saw Samara's name come up on caller ID.

"Hi, Samara," she said. "What do you need?"

CHAPTER 8

When she neared Wesley's office, Lydia slowed her pace. The door was slightly ajar, allowing her to peek inside.

He was there, going through a stack of papers on his mahogany desk. Lydia considered once more how handsome Wesley looked, even wearing the cowboy hat. In fact, he looked downright sexy.

Lydia knocked softly to get his attention.

Wesley glanced up. A smile lit up his gorgeous eyes when he saw her. "C'mon in, darlin'," he said.

"So what do you think of this outfit, Wes?" Lydia asked as she twirled around slowly. "Does it meet with your approval?" She had chosen a pair of jeans, cowboy boots and a tank top beneath a vest.

"You look great," he told her with a grin on his face. "You actually look like you belong on a ranch."

Wesley did not delay getting started.

"These heritage breeds serve as an important genetic resource," he began. "By raising heritage breeds, we are able to maintain variety within our livestock population."

"Why is that important?" Lydia asked as she took notes.

"When heritage breeds become extinct, their unique genes are lost and can't be used to breed new traits into existing livestock breeds," Wesley explained. "Raising heritage livestock can also help preserve valuable traits within the species so that future breeds can endure harsh conditions. For example, our animals are able to survive without the constant doses of antibiotics that are administered to livestock on factory farms."

"Are your animals raised on a pasture?" Lydia inquired.

"They are," he confirmed. "We have several acres for our livestock to roam, and we offer a diversity of grasses to eat."

The more she learned, the more Lydia found the information interesting. She had never heard of or paid attention to the subject of heritage breeding until she read Wesley's profile and several articles in magazines.

"Raising cattle, from my understanding, involves several operations, with each serving a unique role in the process," Lydia stated.

"You're correct," Wesley confirmed. "Beef production represents the largest single segment of American agriculture. You will find that more farms are classified as beef cattle operations than any other type."

She surveyed the cattle as they roamed about. "You have cows and calves, I see."

He nodded. "We maintain a breeding herd of cows that nurture calves every year."

Wesley walked Lydia over to another area.

"Over here is where we place mature calves. They will spend anywhere from four to six months here and are given a balanced diet."

"Until they reach market weight?" she asked.

"You've done your research, I see."

"There's nothing like seeing it firsthand."

"Have I bored you already?" Wesley inquired.

"No, I've actually learned a lot," Lydia responded quickly. "This has been really educational for me. I've been thinking about switching over to organic foods, and you've helped me make up my mind. Thank you."

"What do you have planned for the next two days?" Wesley asked.

"I don't have anything special planned,"

Lydia answered.

"I still owe you the date that you paid generously for. I'd like to make good on that deal tomorrow. We can leave around ten tomorrow morning — and bring an overnight bag. We are going to Helena for the weekend."

"Wow . . . you really have me intrigued."

He grinned. "That's the idea."

"I don't suppose that you'll give me any details about this trip."

"Pack comfortable clothes, but don't forget to bring something dressy for the evening."

"I was hoping for just a little more information."

He chuckled. "Sorry, that's all I'm telling, lil' lady."

Wesley escorted her to the main house. "I told my mother that you would have some questions for her."

"She doesn't mind talking to me right now?"

"She cleared her calendar to spend some time with you. My mother loves talking about her horses."

Lydia hugged him. "Thanks so much, Wes. For all of this."

"It's my pleasure," he uttered as he opened the front door.

Gwendolyn Webb Broward entered the foyer where they stood talking.

"Hello, Lydia," she said smoothly.

"Mrs. Broward, thank you so much for taking time out of your busy schedule to talk to me. I really appreciate it."

She stood at least five foot nine, Lydia estimated. She was an attractive woman with a welcoming smile to match the warmth of her eyes.

"I thought we could start by the stables. I'd like for you to meet my horses."

"I would love it."

As they walked toward the stables, Gwendolyn glanced over at Lydia and said, "My son appears to have taken a strong interest in you."

"I am also very interested in Wes," she responded truthfully. "I like him a lot."

Gwendolyn smiled then. "I really believe that you will be good for him."

At the stables, Gwendolyn proudly showed off her stock.

"What is the best time of year to breed?" Lydia inquired. "Or does it matter?"

"Oh, it matters," she responded. "Mares have a natural breeding season, which is in the spring. However, there are ways to begin the season earlier by artificially increasing the amount of light."

"What does that do?"

"Sunlight stimulates the receptor centers in the brain, which then triggers the production of reproductive hormones," Gwendolyn explained.

"Is this a normal practice?" Lydia inquired.

Gwendolyn nodded. "It's more common in thoroughbred studs to try and produce foals as close to January 1 as possible. It's the official birthday of all thoroughbred racehorses."

She smiled. "I didn't know that."

"In my opinion, the best time for a foal to be born is between the months of May and July. This is when the most grass is available, and it helps the mare's milk supply."

"Is there a best time for a mare to be pregnant?" Lydia asked as she continued to take notes.

"June through August," Gwendolyn replied.

Before Lydia realized, she and Gwendolyn had spent the past two hours talking about horse breeding and her life as a rancher's wife.

She glanced down at her notes before asking, "Have you ever considered doing something else with your life?"

"I love what I do and horses are my passion," replied Gwendolyn. "Outside of being a wife and a mother, there is nothing else I want to do."

"I think I've taken up enough of your time," Lydia said, checking her watch.

"You don't have to rush off. In fact, I'd like to know a little more about you."

She swallowed hard. Lydia really did not like talking about herself. "What would you like to know?"

"Where are you from? I would say somewhere in New York." Gwendolyn smiled. "I have an ear for accents."

"I'm originally from Syracuse," Lydia said.

"What took you to Los Angeles?"

"My desire to work in entertainment management." She met Gwendolyn's gaze. "It's my passion."

"I suppose you've told Wes about this."

"I have," Lydia confirmed. "I'm sure if things grow serious between us, then we will have to have another conversation. But for now, he doesn't have a problem with it."

Gwendolyn's probing brought turbulent thoughts to the forefront of Lydia's mind, however. She really did care a great deal for Wes, but could she give up her dream for him?

Wesley arrived promptly at ten the next

morning.

"Good morning," Lydia greeted when she opened her door. She was dressed and ready to leave with a large designer tote in hand.

She was wearing a pair of white jeans embellished with silver studs that traveled from the pockets and down the outer seam. Lydia's turquoise top was also adorned with silver studding around the neckline. Fringe fell from the empire waist of the tunic.

"You look nice," he told her.

"Thank you for the compliment. I wasn't really sure how to dress based on the little amount of information you gave me."

His gaze slid over her body, and his approval showed in his eyes.

During the drive to Helena, Wesley asked, "How did it go with my mother?"

"Great," Lydia responded. "She's a really sweet lady."

"My mom really likes you."

"Did she tell you that?" Lydia wanted to know.

Wesley nodded. "She told me that we were good for each other."

"She mentioned the same thing to me. But what do you think, Wes?" Lydia inquired. "Do you feel the same way?"

He stole a quick glance in her direction. "Actually, I do."

Lydia settled back in her seat, a smile forming on her lips. "As much as I hate thinking about it, I will have to leave one day soon."

"I know," Wes responded quietly. "Not saying I'm looking forward to that day at all." After a moment, he said, "Lydia, you know that I don't want you to go."

"I'm not sure I want to leave," she admitted.

Wesley reached over and took her hand in his. "Let's not have this discussion until after we get back to Granger. I don't want any dark clouds hanging over this weekend."

"I agree," she told him.

Upon their arrival to Helena, Wesley announced, "We are going to take a ride into the Old West for the first part of our date."

"I see you've discovered my love for history."

He nodded as he parked the car.

Wesley led her toward a waiting horse-drawn wagon. "I want this day to be special, so I came up with plans that I believe you are gonna love."

He helped her inside.

"This is a wonderful start," Lydia stated. "I can't believe I'm in an authentic horse and wagon."

"The horse is definitely authentic, but the

wagon, I'm afraid, is a replica," Wesley confessed. "I don't think we'd want to ride in one from the 1800s."

"Okay, so it's not authentic, but this is pretty close."

"This is Miner's Alley," Wesley said, indicating a point of interest. "It was considered a miners village from the gold rush days."

"What is that cabin over there?" Lydia inquired.

"That's the old Mack cabin. It was built in 1864 and is one of the last remaining structures that represent Helena's early history."

"I'd like to take a picture of the cabin. Can we stop for a minute or two?"

Smiling, Wesley nodded.

Another couple offered to take a photo of Lydia and Wesley.

She eagerly accepted the offer.

Lydia was in awe of the wildlife she'd seen along the way. She had pictures of a moose, a family of deer and an elk.

"Next on the trail is the Old Fire Tower," Wesley announced. "Built in 1876, it's one of the few remaining fire towers in the United States."

She turned toward him and asked, "So what's next on the trail?"

"I was thinking that we should try our hands at mining," Wesley answered. "My father took us when we were younger, but I didn't find much of anything. Maybe I'll have better luck with you."

"What are we mining for?"

"We may find sapphires in every color, garnets, topaz and citrine. I've heard of diamond finds, but it's very rare."

"Sapphires are my favorite gemstone," Lydia murmured. "My mother gave me a sapphire ring and matching necklace for my sixteenth birthday. I loved it."

"Do you still have it?"

She shook her head no. "The ring was stolen from my room in college. I left it on my desk one day — I was running late and forgot to put it on my finger. My roommate was very social and was always having people over. When I returned to my room, the ring was gone."

"Did you talk to your roommate?"

"Yeah, for all the good it did," Lydia replied. "She defended her friends. The ring was never found and my roommate and I split up. She moved in with her boyfriend, so I had the room to myself."

Lydia snapped photographs of the quaint turn-of-the-century mine that sat on the banks of Hauser Lake. The scenery was made more beautiful by the fact that she was spending time with Wesley. She relaxed, sinking into his cushioning embrace. The mere touch of his hand sent a warning shiver through Lydia.

"Okay, this is where we get off," Wesley said.

"We are actually going to do this?" she asked.

"Yeah."

He picked up a small black bag, prompting Lydia to ask, "What's that?"

"Ziplock bags, rubber gloves, sunblock and a couple of hand towels."

She smiled. "Always prepared, I see."

"What cowboy isn't prepared?"

"This is going to be interesting," Lydia murmured. She was relieved that Wesley had thought to bring gloves because she would've hated ruining her manicure. She was pretty sure they were not going to find anything of value. However, the thrill was in the searching.

"The wooden benches can get hard as the day goes on," Wesley announced. "You may want to sit on one of those towels."

"I'll be fine," she assured him. "I'm not that fragile, Wes."

"There's a cowgirl in you, Lydia. I know it."

"I'm not so sure about that," she responded as she picked up a small metal object. "Okay, I don't have a clue as to what to do with this stuff."

Wesley laughed. "I'll show you."

"Just how many buckets did you purchase?" Lydia glanced down and counted eight pails of dirt.

"I figured we should leave here with something." Wesley pointed and said, "That's your screen and there is a flume. The dirt goes in the screen, which goes in the water. The mud gets washed away in the water. It's that simple."

"It does sound pretty simple." Still, Lydia wasn't sure she was going to be any good at identifying anything of value.

One of the technicians offered a minilesson on gem mining. "Gemstones come in every color from white to black. Garnets can be anywhere from a real glassy red, pink or reddish brown."

Lydia felt the heat of Wesley's gaze on her. She stole a peek at him.

He winked at her and she awarded him a smile.

"Rubies are silky red," the technician was saying. "Sapphires are every other color. Both rubies and sapphires have a crystal formation with six sides."

Lydia did not hear the rest of what the man was saying because her heart was thudding loudly in her chest. Wesley embraced her and planted a kiss on her forehead.

After the technician finished talking, Wesley gave her a pail of dirt and took one for himself. Lydia's excitement waned as she neared the bottom.

"Find anything?" he asked her.

"Nothing but dirt," she responded drily.

By the time she was ready for her third pail, Lydia was more than set to call it a day. She was hot and the wooden bench steadily refused to be kind to her bottom. She finished off her second bottle of water.

Lydia watched Wesley for a moment. He was so involved with mining that he paid no attention to her. He didn't seem to have any more luck than she did.

She reluctantly returned her attention to her own pail of dirt.

Lydia checked the rocks that were left on her screen. She picked up one, surveying it closely. "Wes . . ."

He glanced up. "You find something, darlin'?"

"Um . . . I don't know. Could you take a look?"

"Sure."

Wesley held up the largest stone and then

set it down, picking up another. "Honey, I think you've found a few pieces of garnet."

He signaled for the technician.

"More than one?" Lydia asked. "Are you sure?"

Wesley nodded. "Looks like it to me. Congratulations."

She stood on tiptoe and kissed him.

The technician confirmed that Lydia had indeed found garnets. Her excitement renewed, she was ready to continue mining for more hidden gems.

Wesley was already on his fourth pail. Right before she started on her last one, Lydia caught sight of him checking out a bluish-colored stone in his hand and asked, "Did you find anything?"

He showed it to her.

It was a nice-size crystal structure that was hexagon in shape. "Is this a sapphire?" she asked in a low voice.

"I'm not sure, but I think so."

Wesley slipped it into his ziplock bag.

When they had gone through all of their pails, Lydia had found a moonstone and a citrine while Wesley's largest find was the sapphire, but he also discovered a couple of tiny moonstones and what they both thought could be a ruby.

After washing up in the ladies' room,

Lydia found Wesley was waiting on her.

"Are you hungry?"

"Yes," Lydia responded.

He helped her back into the wagon.

"Where are we going now?"

"I've arranged for a picnic by a running brook. This is how it was done in the Old West."

Lydia was touched beyond words by the amount of thought Wesley had put into planning this day. She had won a cowboy, and he had given her a dream date that only a cowboy could come up with. One of the things she disliked about the men in her past was that they never seemed to have any imagination or creativity. Wesley was spontaneous, and she loved that about him.

He had even selected the perfect spot for a romantic picnic. The secluded area was surrounded by shade trees. A picnic table, complete with a checkered tablecloth and basket of food, awaited them.

"You've thought of everything," Lydia murmured.

"Not everything," he responded. "I forgot to have someone serenade you while you eat."

"I think it would've clashed with your whole Western theme," she said as she reached for a sandwich and handed it to

Wesley. "It would've been a really nice touch though."

Lydia grabbed another sandwich and unwrapped it.

"I still have tonight," Wesley said. "No seduction is complete without a nice, expensive meal."

"Oh, really?" She noted the amused glint in his eye.

"What? You didn't know?"

Lydia laughed. "It doesn't take all this to seduce me."

"Okay, I'm listening," Wesley said as he put down his sandwich.

"Seduction is founded in confidence," she said. "Without inner strength, most men seem to fall back on stupid pickup lines and games to try and trap a woman. Honesty is so much more alluring. I love a man who's grounded, solid and aware of who he is — this is what sets him ahead of the rest.

"So if I wanted to seduce you, what would it take?" Lydia inquired.

"For me, seduction works best when the woman doesn't even realize she is doing anything out of the ordinary," Wesley responded. "For example, the way you lick your lips after eating a strawberry drives me crazy. Then there's the way that you run your fingers through your hair. . . . It's not easy to keep from touching you."

Lydia knew exactly where this conversation was heading. She had to change the subject and quick, she thought as she gratefully took a sip of her soda.

She touched the can to her heated forehead and told herself to get a grip. After a moment, Lydia asked softly, "Wes, what are we doing?"

"Our relationship has deepened and I don't think we should ignore it."

Lydia took a sip of her soda. She wasn't sure how to respond to Wesley's comment. It was true. Their feelings for one another had grown. As far as she was concerned, he was the genuine article.

"Am I alone in this?" he questioned.

She reached over and took his hand. "You are definitely not alone. I care greatly for you, Wes, and I want you in my life." The admission sent a thread of fear through Lydia. What was she thinking? Relationships were challenging, especially long-distance ones. She had to really delve deep within to be sure that this was something she wanted to pursue.

I'm falling in love with Wesley. I don't want to lose him.

There. She'd said it. Not aloud, but it was an admission she had been reluctant to make. However, the thought of giving her heart to someone made her fearful. Perhaps it was the risk. Or the realization that for once in her life Lydia wasn't the one in control.

Wesley gave her hand a gentle squeeze, tearing her away from her thoughts. He leaned close enough for Lydia to feel his breath upon her cheek.

For every cell in her body to quiver with heightened awareness.

Her skin to get goose bumps.

"You are all that I think about, Lydia. Needless to say, I can't see my life without you in it. I know that we have a lot to discuss in terms of your going back to Los Angeles, but we are not going to do that right now. I have something better in mind."

Wesley's lips touched hers.

The smoldering fire within Lydia erupted into a wildfire, raging untamed.

When he pulled away, her gaze shifted to his eyes, and something hot and sultry sparked between them.

Lydia knew she was doomed.

After the picnic, Wesley checked them into a hotel. "I'll give you some time to just relax. We've had a full day and I don't want to overdo it. I made dinner reservations for seven."

Lydia was a tiny bit surprised that he had booked separate rooms for them, but she was also relieved. Although she wanted to feel Wesley's skin against her own, Lydia fought to keep her desires under control. It was still too soon for her to consider having an intimate relationship with Wesley, despite the fires he ignited within her.

She opted to take a long soak in the tub instead of a quick shower to cool her feverish body.

After her bath, Lydia realized just how tired she really was. They had spent the day outside and the sun could be draining, she reasoned.

As she stretched out on the bed, she placed a call to her mother.

"Mama, how are you?" she asked.

"I'm doing okay. How are you? Are you still out of town?"

"Yes, I'm still in Montana." Lydia was thrilled to hear her mother's voice. She didn't like the weariness she heard in her tone, however.

"I guess you'll be doing lots of traveling with this job."

"Some," Lydia stated. "I'd like to try and visit you soon. I miss you, Mama."

"I miss you, too. The post office has me working crazy hours, so you have to let me know way ahead of time when you plan to come home."

"I will. Hopefully, I'll be able to retire you."

"Lydia, I don't want you worrying about me. As long as I have my strength, I don't mind working, honey. You just take care of you."

They talked for a few minutes more before getting off the phone.

She sounds so tired. The thought brought tears to Lydia's eyes.

She fell asleep with her mother still weighing heavily on her mind.

Two hours later, Wesley entered her room wearing dark jeans, a starched denim shirt and cowboy boots. He was a vision as far as Lydia was concerned.

Lydia was dressed in clothes appropriate for a night in L.A., complete with platform-heeled black boots and shiny lip gloss. Outwardly, the couple did not exactly look as if they belonged together, but she didn't care. Her heart knew his, and that was more important than how they looked on the outside.

During dinner, Lydia barely touched her plate. She was enjoying her conversation with Wesley immensely.

"You're not hungry?" Wesley inquired as he pointed toward her plate.

"You hardly touched yours, either," she responded with a soft chuckle. "We've been talking the entire time we've been here."

He leaned back in his chair. "I guess we did cover a lot of territory. We talked about us, our families, your time in L.A., about my life in Granger."

"Good stuff," Lydia said with a grin. She found herself increasingly lost in his deep brown eyes, his gentle manner and his work-honed confidence. Wesley was truly like no man she had ever met before.

"I am committed to making our relationship work," he stated. "It's not often a man comes across a woman as special as you are to me. I'm not going to let you disappear from my life, Lydia. I just want you to know that."

She smiled. "I'm just as committed as you are, Wes."

One look in his eyes and Lydia knew that they would be skipping dessert.

Wesley signaled for the check.

Twenty minutes later, they were back at the hotel and in her room.

He pulled her into his arms.

His lips tasted sweet and heady like the

128

wine, and it took every ounce of strength Lydia had to keep from losing herself with him. Wesley held himself in check, not pushing her at all. He did not attempt to undress her, although she might not have refused him.

After what felt like a blissful eternity, he deepened the kiss, nibbling and tasting her until his breathing was harsh and ragged.

They parted reluctantly.

Having briefly recovered her equilibrium, Lydia felt herself begin to heat up again, from the inside, as Wesley continued to gaze at her. She began to consider that being held in his arms like this all night long wouldn't be a problem. However, deep down, she knew better.

Wesley did, too, because he sat up and said, "I think I'd better find my way to my room. If I stay here any longer . . ."

He did not have to finish his sentence. Lydia and Wesley both knew what would happen if he stayed. She had already made it clear that she wanted to wait. She could not back down now. As much as Lydia wanted Wesley to make love to her, she had to stand her ground.

Lydia had such a warm, loving spirit, and she was always smiling. Wesley loved her sense of humor and the sense of freedom she seemed to have in her life. Not only was she beautiful, but she was intelligent, as well. The more he got to know her, the more he wanted to know about her.

He meant what he'd told her earlier. The undeniable magnetism that was building between them forced Wesley to acknowledge the truth. *I have real feelings for Lydia. I'm beginning to fall in love with her.*

The silent declaration surprised him, but Wesley didn't bother to deny the truth. There was not much point. But as strong as his attraction was to Lydia, he had to rein in his feelings. While they'd found some common ground, they still had very different views of what they wanted for the future.

According to his brother, a relationship between them could never work. Wesley once believed the very same thing. But he had all these conflicting emotions where Lydia was concerned, and he could not just let her walk out of his life.

Too many times, he stayed on the road of what was absolute. Wesley was tired of playing it safe. This time he was going to take a chance. He was going to take a risk for love.

Lydia was worth it. What he felt for her was worth it.

Jameson would call him a fool, but Wesley

didn't care. He had his own life to live, and Jameson had his own living to do.

Wesley's whole world had been enriched by Lydia's presence. He was a better man because of her, and he was thankful. Even if the relationship fizzled out, Wesley vowed that he would always be grateful for having met Lydia.

Lydia could hear a sea of low murmurings all around her when she and Wesley arrived at the Dillons' barbecue the following weekend at the Double D Ranch. Maggie had forewarned her about the angry glares sent her way from several of the women present.

"There you are," Maggie shouted from across the yard. "I was wondering when you were going to get here."

"Looks like you two are becoming good friends," Wesley said in a low voice.

"She's been great to me," Lydia whispered. "Maggie's never treated me like an outsider."

"Wes, bring Lydia over here," Maggie called out. "I want to introduce her to some people."

"Here we go," Wes muttered with a chuckle.

Lydia pretended not to notice all the attention focused on her and Wesley. Instead, she decided to enjoy this time with Wesley. Her feelings for him were growing more and more each day.

The hair on the back of her neck stood up.

She glanced around until her eyes landed on Jameson. Lydia boldly met his gaze and smiled.

He smiled back, and then turned away from her.

She received a warmer reception from Gwendolyn. "Lydia, how lovely you look."

The two women embraced.

"How are you, Mrs. Broward?"

"I'm fine," she responded graciously.

"Have I told you just how beautiful you look?" Wesley whispered when his mother walked away.

Lydia looked up at him. "No, I don't think you did. I'm pretty sure I would've remembered."

Wesley loved that Lydia always wore a genuine smile. Just being around her brightened up even the sunniest day, as far as he was concerned. It was one of the qualities that attracted him to her in the first place. His eyes traveled to her shapely legs, the sight of them stirring something in him as always.

A woman pressed her body against him as she passed him.

"Sorry, ma'am," he uttered.

It wasn't always easy to avoid distractions. Wesley constantly had to deal with overly aggressive women who practically threw themselves at him. His gaze traveled back to where Lydia was sitting. He watched her as she tilted her head back in laughter.

"You must really like her," Laney observed aloud. "I've never seen you pay so much attention to one woman."

"She's special to me."

"I think it's real nice . . . the way you look at her."

For a moment, Wesley thought he glimpsed a shadow of sadness pass over his sister's face.

Before he could ask the question on his mind, Laney said, "I've got to ask Maggie about something."

She was gone before he could utter a response. Something was definitely going on with Laney.

He was about to go after her, but Lydia stopped him. "Where are you running off to?"

Wesley broke into a grin. "Nowhere, darlin'."

After the barbecue, they ended up back at

his place.

"This is such a wonderful house," Lydia told him. "There's so much history here within these walls."

Wesley reached over, pulling her closer to him. "What I cherish most about this place is that it was built on love. There was a lot of it in this house. I want my children and their children to know how much love exists in here."

Lydia stood on tiptoe and pulled his head down to hers, kissing him.

Wesley responded, matching her kiss for kiss.

Desire ignited in her belly, causing her to pull away reluctantly. "I'm sorry, Wes. It's too easy for us to get carried away."

Their gazes locked and both of them could see the attraction mirrored in the other's eyes.

"I won't let anything happen if you're not ready, sweetheart." Wesley pulled her back into his arms.

He kissed her again, lingering, savoring every moment.

Her emotions whirled.

Blood pounded in her brain, leaped from her heart and made her knees tremble.

Lydia kissed him with a hunger that belied

her outward calm, and she was unashamed by her own eager response.

CHAPTER 9

Lydia had fallen asleep in Wesley's arms on the sofa the night before. It was not her intention to spend the night, but when she woke up, it was sunrise and she was alone.

Wesley strolled out of his bedroom a few minutes later. "Morning, sleepyhead."

"Why didn't you wake me up?" she asked.

"You were sleeping so peacefully, I didn't want to disturb you."

He was dressed in a pair of sweatpants and T-shirt, which stunned Lydia. "I didn't think you owned anything but denim," she said.

Wesley chuckled. "It's good I can still surprise you." He pointed toward the kitchen. "Are you hungry?"

"A little."

"I can whip up some scrambled eggs, bacon and toast," Wesley stated. "If you're craving something more, then I'll have to have Rusty whip it up for you."

"No, that's fine," Lydia murmured. She searched for her purse and said, "I need to freshen up."

"There's a brand-new toothbrush in the bathroom," he told her.

"Thanks, but I keep one in my purse," she responded.

Lydia returned to the kitchen a few minutes later, refreshed. "Can I help with anything?"

Wesley gave her a sidelong glance. "Can you cook?"

"No, you didn't," she uttered with a short laugh. "I know you did not just ask me that. The man with the cook on call twenty-four/seven."

He handed her a pack of bacon. "Hey, you are staying in a hotel. I don't know what your culinary talents are — haven't had the chance to experience them. As for Rusty, he works for my parents."

"How many times a week do you eat at the main house?"

"A lot."

She laughed. "Enough said. Now step aside so that I can fry up this bacon."

"Yes, ma'am."

Lydia could feel the heat of Wesley's gaze on her as she cooked up the bacon. That task completed, she made toast while he scrambled the eggs.

Is this what it would be like to be married to this man?

She shook the thought away. It was dangerous to let ideas like this rush to her mind, her heart warned.

While she ate, Lydia surveyed the house. The upper loft included an additional sleeping area and library for guests. She loved the way the spaciousness, peacefulness and warmth echoed throughout. Lydia understood what Wesley meant when he said the house was built on love.

"What's it really like to be a modern-day cowboy?" she inquired as she reached for her orange juice.

"Ranching has become more efficient in this age of technology," Wesley stated. He wiped his mouth on his napkin. "There are still a lot of things done the traditional way, but with a cell phone, truck or a trailer, a lot can be done faster."

She gave him a sidelong glance. "In what way?"

"Look at those guys out there," he said, pointing toward the window. "This week, they moved a set of cows and calves ten miles to pasture. They left at the crack of dawn and drove them on horseback. Fifty years ago, they would have driven the cattle

138

and then made the ride back home. They would've packed lunches and tried to make it back by dinner."

Wesley paused a moment before continuing. "Nowadays, we meet them with a truck and trailer at the end point, bringing them back here for lunch, and the horses are spared the return trip on foot. These days, we are able to complete two or three trips before dark."

"Wow . . . That's certainly progress."

He nodded in agreement. "I have to admit that I enjoy the work a lot more now than when I was growing up."

"How does your grandfather feel about today's technology in ranching?"

"He was a bit resistant at first, but he has adapted well," Wesley admitted. "Grandpa used to tell me and my brother that we had to learn to ranch the old way before we could fully appreciate the land and all that we have."

"Was he right?"

Wesley smiled. "Yes, ma'am, I think he was."

"I have to say that you're very different from your brother," Lydia stated. "One look at him and I can tell immediately that he's a cowboy. If I'd met you in Los Angeles . . . *cowboy* would never come to mind unless you were dressed like one."

Wes downed the last of his coffee and then poured himself another cup. "I'm not sure how I'm supposed to respond to that."

She chuckled. "It's a compliment, Wes."

Lydia got up and walked over to the window in the kitchen. "I saw your mother's horses at the main stables. I didn't know that you have one, as well."

"Actually, my brother and I share this one," Wesley responded. "This one was the original stable. It caught fire when my dad was a young boy. I had it rebuilt maybe five years ago."

"How many horses do you own?" Lydia asked as they neared the stables. "I think I counted at least a dozen when your mother gave me a tour."

"I have four," he responded. "Laney and my mother have ten horses. They sold two of them last week at the auction."

Wesley took her by the hand and led her into the stable. "C'mon, I'll introduce you to them."

She relished the feel of his skin touching hers.

"This is Queenie Blue. She's a twelve-year-old blue roan mare."

"She's gorgeous," Lydia murmured.

"And this is Shadow."

"Nice to meet you, Shadow," she said. "You are a pretty horse. I bet you're a sweetie."

"Right here, we have Spartan. Shadow is his foal." He pointed to his right. "Over there is Sweet Mac."

Lydia chuckled at the name.

"Have you ever ridden a horse?" Wesley wanted to know.

"I rode a pony when I was about five or six."

He laughed.

"I'm pretty sure that there's not much difference between the two," Lydia stated.

"Would you like to take a ride? I want to show you the rest of the ranch."

"Sure," she responded with a smile.

"Shadow is a really calm horse," Wesley told her. "She's perfect for you."

He helped her up.

"Okay, I don't remember it being like this," Lydia said. "This saddle is not very comfortable." She held the reins together in the palm of her left hand.

"When you want her to turn, move your hand to either side," Wesley instructed. "When you do that, you're controlling Shadow's head. Control her head and her body will follow."

Lydia wasn't afraid, but she felt twinges of

anxiety at the thought of riding a horse for the first time in her life. She recounted Wesley's instructions to apply a downward pressure with her feet in the stirrups — this was supposed to keep her from all of the bouncing up and down in the saddle.

"How are you doing, lil' lady?" he asked after they had ridden for about ten minutes.

"Okay, I think," Lydia responded with a grimace. "This saddle isn't at all comfortable, Wes."

He looked back at her. "Try standing up from time to time — this should help relieve some of the pain."

She shook her head no. "I'd rather focus on riding right now. I'm not ready to try anything like standing."

"Why don't we head back?" Wesley suggested, turning his horse around. "You're going to be sore after your ride, and it's going to be even worse tomorrow."

"Let's keep going. I'll be fine," she assured him.

Cool, moist air washed in as they rode past the main house. It had rained sometime in the night, but the air still smelled sweet, fresh and alive. Lydia loved mornings like this. She would miss this when she returned to Los Angeles.

"Are you okay?" he inquired.

"Yes." She gave him a tight smile.

Wesley broke into a grin. "I told you that you were going to be sore."

Her bottom was aching, but Lydia refused to give in to the pain. She wanted to prove to Wesley that she could survive life on a ranch.

But for what purpose?

The next morning, Lydia's body screamed in protest as she eased out of bed and padded barefoot to the shower.

She showered and dressed in a pair of sweats. It was the only clothing that felt comfortable. Her hair was damp from her shower, so Lydia allowed it to hang freely in soft curls.

She walked gingerly over to the sofa and eased herself down. Lydia had just reached for her laptop when a sudden knock on her door caught her by surprise.

She muttered a curse at the thought of having to get up.

The knock persisted.

Grunting in pain, Lydia made her way to the door and yanked it open.

"Good morning," Wes greeted with a smile on his face. "I thought I'd come check on you. I wanted to make sure you survived your first horse ride."

"I didn't think I'd be this sore. I came home and soaked in the tub yesterday." Lydia made a face. "I don't know if I'll ever get back on another horse."

"The second day is always the worst. That's why I made an appointment for you with Calamity Jane's Spa and Salon. My mother and sister rave about their services."

Lydia was both surprised and touched by his gesture. "Really? Wes, this is very thoughtful of you."

"Hopefully, after a day of pampering, you'll feel like having dinner with me tonight."

"Spa or no spa, I would love to have dinner with you," she responded with a smile.

"So all is forgiven then?"

"Yes, all is forgiven," Lydia told him.

He planted a kiss on her forehead. "I'll take you to the spa. I'm not sure you should be driving in your condition."

She pushed him toward the door. "I'm not that fragile, Wes. I'll see you tonight."

When he left, she groaned softly. "I am never getting on another horse as long as I live."

Within the hour, Lydia was on a table with her eyes closed, enjoying a hot-stone massage. She had passed by the spa a few times but never once thought to treat herself to the myriad of spa services offered.

Now I see why Samara's so addicted to what she calls her rejuvenation treatments. This is heavenly.

Her mother's birthday was coming up in a few months, and she knew exactly what she wanted to do for her. She was going to take her to a spa. Everyone needed to experience this journey of health and beauty, Lydia decided.

It amazed her that somehow Wesley always seemed to know what she needed. Lydia wondered if this was what it was like for soul mates.

After her hot-stone massage, she opted for a mud treatment for her hands and feet while one of the attendants gave her a warm scalp massage.

Lydia strolled out of the spa feeling like a new woman, renewed and filled with anticipation.

"You look stunning," Wesley said.

He then reached across the table and kissed her on the lips.

Lydia broke into a smile. "I suppose you are partly responsible for my transformation. I will be frequenting Calamity Jane's while I'm here in Granger. It was truly an amazing experience."

Lydia did not add that this was the first time she had ever been to a spa. Although Samara frequented them every other day, she had never once invited Lydia to join her.

"I'm glad you enjoyed yourself," he responded.

"I did. I feel so much better, too."

"I don't think we can ignore the obvious," Wesley announced. "What we feel for one another is not something fleeting."

Lydia wiped her mouth on the edge of a napkin. "I agree."

He met her gaze. "I told you before that I was not going to just let you walk out of my life. I meant it."

"Wes, I want you to know that I've learned a lot about ranching — and even about myself — from you. If someone had told me six months ago that I would be here in Granger, Montana . . . I would've burst out laughing."

"How do you feel about Granger now?"

"It's a really beautiful place to live. I have to admit that I had no idea that Montana was so picturesque." She chuckled. "I sound like a tourist, don't I?"

Wesley laughed and nodded. "But it's fine. Since Laney won that gold medal, people from all over have been visiting the town

146

and inquiring about purchasing property. It's a good thing on one hand, but on the other . . ."

"You don't sound happy about this," she commented. "Isn't this a good thing?"

He gave a slight shrug. "I have mixed feelings about it, but I don't want to talk about that right now. I want to talk about us."

He had her full attention.

"I am ready to commit to you, Lydia," Wesley stated. "There is not another woman for me."

"Are you sure about this?" she asked. "Things are fine between us just the way that they are."

Wesley shook his head no. "I want more."

"In truth, so do I," Lydia told him. "I haven't wanted to say it out loud because . . . Wes, do you really believe that we can build a relationship long distance?"

"If we're completely committed to one another, I believe anything is possible. Before I met you, my answer would've been no, it won't work, but now . . . you've changed my perspective on life." He reached across the table and took her hand in his.

"I never imagined in a million years that I could be this happy," she murmured. "Don't get me wrong. I'm a happy person, but it's never been like this." Lydia gave a slight shrug. "I guess I sound silly."

"Believe it or not, I know exactly what you mean," he responded.

"Wes, I want you to know that I don't expect you to walk away from the ranch," Lydia stated. "I will support whatever you decide to do."

"I appreciate that," he told her. "With all of the tourists coming to town and outsiders trying to buy up land — things are gonna change around here. I'm just not sure it's gonna be for the best."

"You mentioned earlier how you have mixed feelings about this." Lydia took a sip of her water. "Maggie isn't really thrilled, either."

"I actually have a piece of property up for sale, but I've been reluctant to seriously pursue any offers. I bought this ranch in Hastings about four years ago but haven't done anything with it. It's beautiful land with a lake. Ten acres with another four acres of trees."

She shifted in her chair. "Why do you want to sell it?"

"I bought it with the idea that I would breed more heritage animals, but right now, I'm contemplating my future in ranching."

"So, you don't want to do this anymore?"

"It's not something I want to do forever,"

he admitted. "I don't want to see good land go to waste, so I think it's best to sell."

"Makes sense to me," Lydia murmured. "You are very good at what you do, Wes, but if it's not your passion, then maybe it is time to make a change. For some people, staying in the family business is the easy way to surf through life. It's more of a challenge to find a place where you fit in or discover what you love to do."

"So what do you think I should do?" Wesley inquired.

"You really want to know?"

He gave a slight nod.

"Wes, if I were you, I'd get a job outside of ranching. I can tell you that hunting for employment sucks, but this is exactly why you should do it. The process is humbling because on one level, you are asking someone to pay you to work so you can eat. On another level, it requires understanding yourself well enough to talk about your dreams, your strengths and your weaknesses. Wes, you need to experience what it is like to ask for a day off from someone who doesn't love you. Job hunting is a rite of passage, and if you don't go through it, you risk stunted growth."

"I don't think I've ever looked at job hunting from this perspective. Strangely, it makes perfect sense to me."

"I've heard people often say how much they regret not taking enough risks. I intend to live my life to the fullest," Lydia said. "Wes, you need to make sure that staying in the family business will not make you wish later that you were a risk taker."

"Risks are different for everyone," Wesley interjected.

"You're right," Lydia replied. "But have you found something that scared you — yet you did it anyway?"

Her words made Wesley pause for thought. "Nothing I can think of."

"Establishing yourself independently from your family can be scary, Wes, but it's what you need to do. Get off the ranch and see the world. After that, you will be able to see yourself more clearly. Whether you decide to stay in the family business or leave to do something else — you will be able to make the decision honestly."

"Beautiful and wise," Wesley uttered. "A perfect combination."

She acknowledged the compliment with a bright smile. "What's the first thing you would do if you had the opportunity?"

"I'd go to Europe," he told her. "I've always wanted to travel. Just never really had the time."

After he paid the check, they left the restaurant and headed back to the hotel to enjoy the rest of the evening.

Lydia turned on the television, but their passion for one another took over and they made out like high school kids on the sofa.

When Wesley finally left her hotel room, Lydia's lips were tender from his passion-filled kisses. Her body temperature hadn't cooled yet, so she decided to take a bubble bath, hoping to ease some of the pent-up tension she felt. No other man's touch had ever left her burning with desire.

CHAPTER 10

"Wes has been wonderful," Lydia told Samara over the phone. "I spent a couple of days on the ranch with him and his family. They are all so nice. They shared so much of their lives with me. I have several pages of notes for you. Would you like me to email them to you?"

"What else have you found out about them? Anything that doesn't have to do with ranching?"

"Samara, there really isn't anything more to learn about Wes and his family. They are of high moral character and upstanding people. None of them have criminal records."

"I read somewhere that Wesley's parents had an arranged marriage. Is this true?"

"I don't know, but I highly doubt it," Lydia responded. "You only have to see them together to know that they deeply love one another."

"Maybe that's what they want you to see," Samara retorted.

Lydia was stunned by her response. "Why do you say that?"

"It's not important."

She bit back her frustration with Samara. When her boss did things like this, it grated Lydia's nerves.

"Everybody has a skeleton or two in their closet," Samara stated. "I'm just curious about the ones hanging in the Browards' closets."

"What would this have to do with a movie role? I'd like to know what you've gotten me into."

"They come across as the perfect family. I'm just trying to humanize them — that's all."

"You make it sound as if the movie is about the Browards."

"It's not," Samara responded. "Lydia, I don't expect you to understand. I'm a perfectionist when it comes to acting and I like to learn everything — the good and the bad — about a person if I'm using them to research a role."

Lydia was not comfortable breaking Wesley's confidence. She did not want to betray him in that way.

"I don't think I can get what you're looking for," she told Samara. "If I keep asking questions, especially personal ones, Wes is going to get suspicious."

"All you have to do is get close to him, Lydia. You're a pretty girl. . . . Just let nature take its course."

"I hope you're not suggesting that I sleep with Wes," Lydia uttered. "Because I'm not going to do that."

"It's not what I'm saying at all, Lydia," Samara responded. "I just thought that he might be attracted to you, so why not flirt around a little?"

Although she and Wesley were closer than ever, Lydia chose not to disclose their relationship to Samara. She did not relish keeping secrets from her boss, but Lydia was afraid that it might lead to questions she was not prepared to answer.

Lydia had vowed never to come near Shadow again, but Wesley convinced her to try riding a second time. It had taken a lot of kisses and pleading to get her to consider his request, but she finally gave in.

Wesley wanted to give her a more in-depth view of what his life was like as a rancher. Lydia needed to know so that she could determine whether or not she really wanted to be a part of his life. She was a city girl, which was a much different way of life from a woman growing up in Granger.

He met Lydia at the car and greeted her with a kiss. "I hope it's not too early for you."

"Getting up at four in the morning — no, it's not too early," she responded with a short laugh. "I'm usually turning over at this time."

Wesley chuckled. "Hey, you wanted an insider's view of ranching."

"That I did," Lydia admitted. "Getting up with the chickens must make for a long day."

"Most days we are always so busy, it actually seems more that there aren't enough hours to get everything done."

Lydia walked beside him toward the stables. "I can see how much you love your horses, this place and your family," she said. "You really have a strong connection to this land."

"We are a very close-knit family," Wesley admitted. "This will always be home to me, but like you said, I need to experience another way of life."

"Doing so may bring you right back to Granger," Lydia said. "But you'll have peace of mind because you will know for sure that this is where you belong." She paused a moment before asking, "Have you discussed any of this with your family?"

Wesley nodded. "I've talked with my grandpa some, but that's about it. He pretty much told me the same thing you did."

"Try lots of things until you find the one thing that you are passionate about," she said. "Then you'll know."

He gave her a smile that warmed her to the core.

"I like that you're very easy to talk to, Lydia."

"I'm also a great listener." She took his hand in her own. "Wes, I've been in this same situation as you. I had no idea what I really wanted to do until now."

"Do you enjoy your job as a personal assistant?" he asked.

His question caught her off guard. "I like what I do," Lydia answered, "but it's just a stepping-stone. I have plans to own my own entertainment management firm one day. Hopefully, this stint as a personal assistant will open the door to landing a job in entertainment."

"Sounds like you know what you really want." Wes was taken aback by her response. He had not expected her to have such long-term plans. He reminded himself that she was nothing like him when it came to goals in life. Lydia knew what she wanted and she set her mind to achieve her dreams.

"I do," Lydia stated. "I've known since college, but it's not an easy path. I'm not a quitter, so I'll take it one day at a time."

"I admire your determination." Wesley could not help but wonder where he fit into her life. Would she be willing to give up her dream to be with him? It was not a question he was prepared to ask.

They shared a smile.

Twenty minutes later, Wesley rode out of the stables ahead of Lydia. He glanced back over his shoulder. "Are you coming?"

"I'm right behind you," she responded. "Shadow and I had to have a serious talk."

"It wasn't Shadow's fault," Wesley stated. "I bought you a new saddle. It should be a little more comfortable for you."

"I think I have calluses on my bottom from the last time, so I should be good," she retorted.

Wesley threw back his head and laughed.

They caught up with the cowboys leading the cattle to pasture.

She had chosen a perfect day for shadowing Wesley. The sun was shining bright and the temperature comfortable.

Lydia pulled her hat down to block more of the sunlight.

She pulled up beside Wesley.

"Hanging in there?" he inquired.

"Yeah," Lydia responded. "I can't believe I'm actually on a cattle drive."

"I can hardly believe it myself," Wesley said with a chuckle.

She sent him a sharp glare.

"We will be trailing two hundred and fifty cow and calf pairs," he announced. "Today's ride will cover the south section of the allotment, but before a cattle drive can take place, the cowhands have to round them up."

"Is that what we're waiting on?"

He nodded.

"This is so exciting," she gushed. Lydia never could have imagined she would be so ecstatic over a cattle run.

"Let's see if you still feel this way by the end of the day," Wesley commented.

He introduced her to a man he referred to as a point rider.

"Okay, what's a point rider?" she asked.

"He rides at the front of the herd," Wesley explained. "The cowboy riding the rear is called a drag rider. Then there is the flank rider. He rides at the sides of the herd to keep them from spreading out."

"I suppose you would be considered the trail boss, then."

Wesley raised his cowboy hat to look at her.

She smiled. "I've been doing some research."

"Okay, then tell me what a swing rider is," he challenged.

Lydia searched her memory. She couldn't recall if she'd come across anything about a swing rider. She decided to just take a guess. "He keeps the herd heading in the right direction. You know . . . swing to the right . . . swing to the left. . . ."

Wesley laughed. "Yeah. Something like that."

She was surprised. "You mean I was right? I totally guessed on that one."

"I know," he responded. "It was a pretty good guess."

The cattle rounded up, they were ready to go.

The ride was easier on Lydia this time around. "Shadow, you are a sweetheart," she told the horse as she patted her neck.

Five hours later, Lydia and Wesley entered his house, tired and hungry.

"I don't know what that is, but it smells wonderful," she commented.

"Rusty's been here," Wesley stated. "I guess we've been spared cold sandwiches.

Looks like he cooked up a hot lunch for us."

Lydia's mouth watered at the sight of the roasted chicken, mashed potatoes, steamed broccoli and corn bread.

She washed her hands in the kitchen sink while Wesley went to the bathroom to clean up.

When he returned, Lydia had prepared plates of food for them.

"Rusty is a dynamic cook," she said when they finished eating. "I'm sure I've put on five pounds just from this meal."

Lydia pushed away from the table and rose to her feet.

Wesley did the same. "You look fine to me."

He grabbed her as she was about to walk past him. Wesley leaned forward and kissed her.

His kiss was slow and thoughtful and sent spirals of desire racing through Lydia.

Weakened by his yearning for her, Wesley pulled away, saying, "Sweetheart, we are going to have to stop."

"I know . . . but I don't want to," she moaned. The kiss had left her weak and a bit confused.

Wesley kissed the top of her head. "Lydia,

you have my flesh screaming for you right now."

She groaned in protest. "Why did you just pull away?"

"You're on the job, remember?" This was not the real reason Wesley was holding back. The truth was that his feelings for her were special. She was special. Lydia challenged him in a way that no other woman ever had; she motivated him to live up to a better version of himself.

"Oh, yeah."

"There's always tonight," he murmured.

She smiled in response.

Although Wesley had not admitted it to himself, he could no longer deny his feelings for Lydia. He was thoroughly and completely in love with her. This was not something that had been in his game plan, but he welcomed it, because Wesley believed that Lydia was the woman for him.

They went to the Shank of the Evening.

"I can't believe that you wanted to come back here," Wesley stated. He took a swig of his beer.

"I like this place," she responded.

He gave her a sidelong glance. "Really?"

Lydia nodded. "Let's dance."

Wesley rose to his feet and escorted her to

the crowded dance floor.

After the third song, Lydia gave in to her thirst. "I need a drink."

They left the dance floor.

Wesley walked her to their table and signaled the waitress to bring another round of drinks.

"Do you have any plans on Sunday?" he asked her.

"I'm not doing anything."

"I would like you to join us for a Broward Sunday dinner."

Lydia broke into a smile. "Really?"

He nodded. "It's time my family really had a chance to get to know you."

She met his gaze. "Why do you say that?"

"It's no secret that I have feelings for you. I want them to see what a great person you are."

"Family approval," she murmured. "Don't worry. You're going to have to meet my mom one day soon."

Wesley finished off his beer. "Feel like dancing?"

Lydia nodded. "I like this song."

They left the Shank of the Evening an hour later and headed to her hotel suite.

He pulled her into his arms. "I love being with you, Lydia."

"I feel the same way," she responded with

a smile. "You're not making it easy for me to go back to L.A."

"Good. I really don't want you to leave."

"Let's not focus on my leaving. I want to enjoy what time we have together."

Wesley agreed before planting a kiss on her lips.

The mere touch of his lips against her own ignited a sensuous flood of warmth through her body. Lydia ached for Wesley's touch, but her mind cautioned her to slow down. She did not want to rush into a physical relationship with him.

Lydia considered making love a bonding experience that she did not want to share with just anyone. Wesley was special to her, but she intended to let more time pass before jumping into bed with him.

"What are you thinking about?"

Wesley's voice cut into her thoughts. Lydia gazed at him and said, "You make me feel things I haven't felt in a long time. Whatever this is, I don't want to rush it."

He nodded in understanding. "I'm not going anywhere, Lydia. You're very special to me."

She reached over and took his hand in her own. "Thank you, Wes."

He was a gentleman, and it was a quality she both loved and admired in him.

■ ■ ■ ■

"You're here again?" Jameson asked when he strode into the family room and found Lydia sitting on the sofa. "I guess I really shouldn't be surprised."

"Hello to you, too," Lydia responded coolly. It was obvious to her that Wesley's brother did not like her, for whatever reason. "I was invited for dinner."

He eyed her for a moment before saying, "I'm sorry. I didn't mean to be rude."

"Yes, you did," Lydia responded. She was not about to let him off that easily. "I don't know why you have a problem with me, Jameson. I haven't done anything to you."

"Why did you come to Granger, Miss Emerson?" he questioned.

"I'm here to do some research, but I'm sure Wes has already told you this."

Jameson shrugged in nonchalance. "He seems to believe you, but I'm afraid that I'm not buying your *story.*"

Lydia forced herself to remain steady beneath his gaze. "It's the truth," she muttered.

"How long will you be staying in our little town?"

She folded her arms across her chest. "I'm

not sure, Jameson. Why does it matter to you?"

"Because my brother has taken an interest in you — someone we know nothing about."

"Wes is a grown man," she told him. "I'm sure he can handle himself."

"What are you after?"

"I'm not after anything, Jameson."

"What's going on?" Wesley interjected as he walked up on them. "Am I interrupting something?" he asked as he looked from his brother to Lydia.

Jameson shot her a tight smile before saying, "No, you're not interrupting anything. I was just getting to know Miss Emerson. Y'all enjoy the rest of your evening."

Lydia was relieved when Jameson left. He made her uncomfortable and she did not enjoy being around him. She knew that he didn't trust her — he'd made that much very clear from the beginning.

A part of her worried that he would go as far as trying to hire a private investigator to look into her past. He seemed very protective of Wesley.

"What's wrong, darling?"

Lydia glanced over at Wesley and forced a smile. "Everything is fine. Your brother is a very interesting person."

"He's been through a lot. Trust doesn't

come easily for him."

She nodded in understanding.

"Before I forget, my parents are hosting a cocktail party next weekend and I'd like you to be my date," Wesley announced. "The theme is the Roaring '20s."

"It sounds like fun," she responded with a grin. "I'd be honored to be your date, but I have to find the perfect outfit."

The more time she spent with Wesley, the more she wanted to be in his presence. They never seemed to tire of one another, which pleased her. But in the back of her mind she wondered when Samara would demand that she return to Los Angeles.

She stole a peek at Wesley. It was going to be so hard to say goodbye to him. They had already discussed that he would fly to L.A. every other weekend, but this would work only if she were home. Who knew where Samara would have her go next? Normally, her weekends were free unless Samara was entertaining.

"What are you thinking about?" Wesley asked, cutting into her thoughts.

"I'm thinking about what I'm going to wear to such an extravagant event," Lydia responded. "I heard a couple of women talking about it at the hotel when I first checked in, but only in passing. Apparently, it's supposed to be the party of the year."

Wesley laughed. "I'm sure it's nothing like the parties you're used to attending."

"I haven't attended many Hollywood parties," she stated. "I'm just the personal assistant. I worked the parties that were hosted by my boss, so I didn't really get to enjoy them."

"Do you have any idea how much longer you will be in town?" he wanted to know.

"Two or three weeks at the most," Lydia responded. "But I won't know for sure until I speak with my boss."

"I guess I'll have to make plans to visit Los Angeles at that time."

She met his gaze. "You mean it, Wes. You're going to fly to L.A. with me?"

He nodded. "I told you. I just can't let you walk out of my life, Lydia."

Gwendolyn walked into the large dining room, which had lovely hardwood floors and enormous windows adorned with rich, emerald-green custom curtains.

"Rusty kept the menu to himself," Gwendolyn announced. "He said he was making something special for dinner."

"I'm sure whatever the man cooks will be delicious," Wesley's grandfather stated. He glanced in Lydia's direction and said,

"You're in for a treat, young lady."

"Rusty really outdid himself tonight," Wesley said as he pulled out a chair for her to sit down.

He sat down in the empty chair beside her.

They were served seafood croquettes and prawns with garlic for starters.

"This is so good," she whispered to Wesley.

"If Rusty was a woman, I'd marry her," Charles Broward stated with a hearty chuckle. "My May . . . she could cook, but I'm afraid Rusty would win this round."

"I don't think Grandma would be real happy with you for saying that," Laney said.

"She'd be mad as fire," Charles responded with a shrug. "Don't make it any less true."

Rusty's main entrée was monkfish with grilled vegetables and rice with mushrooms. For dessert, there was a sweet potato pie.

Lydia was extremely conscious of Jameson's gaze on her. He was studying her every move. She couldn't help but wonder why he seemed so interested in his brother's love life. She also noticed that Steven seemed to be watching her, as well.

She never spent much time around people of privilege on a personal level, but Lydia was curious if they were all so protective of one another as the Browards were. She didn't care about their wealth and wasn't impressed by it, either. Lydia's interest was completely in the man and not his wallet.

"I suppose you plan on bringing Lydia to the cocktail party," Jameson stated when Wesley walked back into the house. "I have to tell you that I'm kinda surprised that you are still seeing her. Especially after she lied to you about her real identity. Wes, how can you trust her?"

"She's the woman I want in my life, and yes, she's coming to the cocktail party with me," Wesley confirmed. "And I do trust her."

"You two seem to be getting pretty close," his mother interjected. "Jameson, I think you're being too hard on Lydia. She really is a lovely girl."

"She's a great person," Wesley stated. "I enjoy spending time with her, regardless of what my brother thinks."

"What are you going to do when it's time for Lydia to leave?" Laney asked. "You haven't forgotten that she's going back to Los Angeles after she finishes her research."

Wesley met his sister's gaze. "I don't know. Right now, I don't want to think about Lydia's leaving. I would rather enjoy the time we have together."

"I hope you're not rushing into anything with this girl," Jameson uttered.

"Leave Wes alone," Laney stated. "If he wants to be with Lydia, it's his choice and there's nothing you can do about it. Why don't you concentrate on finding someone who can get you out of that sour disposition of yours?"

She rushed out of the room.

Jameson and Wesley both looked stunned by Laney's outburst.

"I don't want to see you played for a fool."

"Jameson, I appreciate your concern, but you don't have to worry. I'm okay."

"I hope you will be able to feel the same way six months from now."

"Big brother, I'm afraid I have to agree with Laney," Wesley stated. "I think you need a woman."

CHAPTER 11

"Things must be going great with you and Wes," Maggie said as she searched through a rounder of dresses. "You two are inseparable."

"I feel like we're getting so much closer," Lydia stated. "I have to say that as much as I'm looking forward to going home, I'm not exactly thrilled about leaving Wes. I really care for him, Maggie. He's already planning to come to L.A. with me when I have to go back. It's just a visit though."

"I do hope that you know Wes is not going to move to Los Angeles. His whole life is here." Maggie selected a dress and held it against her body. "Have you considered moving to Granger?"

Lydia did not comment, because no one else knew of Wesley's conflicting feelings in regards to ranching.

She eyed a flapper-style dress on the rack to her left. "Maggie, our relationship hasn't progressed to the point where we have to think about anyone relocating."

"From the looks of things, I'd say you aren't too far off, sugar."

"I'm just taking it one day at a time, Maggie." She held up the flapper dress. "What do you think about this one?"

"Sugar, it's perfect for you."

Lydia walked over to a mirror and eyed her reflection. "I like it."

Maggie followed her. "Add a feathered headband and you're all set for the party."

She glanced over her shoulder. "How should I wear my hair?"

"Finger waves," Maggie responded. "I think I'm going to do the same. Only I'm going to have a peacock feather."

"I thought you were still looking for a dress."

"I am."

Lydia chuckled. "Yet you've already decided on the headpiece."

"I wanted to have a Roaring '20s–theme wedding, but Dane would not go for it. He wanted a traditional church wedding. I loved him, so I didn't fight him on it. I bought that headpiece for our wedding." She chuckled. "You should have seen his face when I told him that we had to dress up for this party."

"What's he wearing?"

"He said he was gonna wear whatever cowboys wore during that time period."

Lydia gave a short laugh. "I love it."

"Do you know what Wes plans to wear?"

"He told me to think Great Gatsby," she responded. "I don't know how I'm going to act seeing him without a pair of jeans on. I almost forgot that he had on a tuxedo when I met him. But then, the man can wear a paper bag and still look good in it."

"Amen to that, sugar."

Gwendolyn and Steven Broward transformed the main house into a 1920s theme for the cocktail party. White fairy lights were strung up and the other lighting dimmed to create an illumination effect. They had chosen a black-and-white color scheme with accents of red and silver. The table centerpieces featured beautiful red roses arranged on candelabra.

Lydia felt like Cinderella at the ball.

Well, Cinderella at a Roaring '20s party.

The elite of Montana were in attendance at the elegant cocktail party hosted by Steven and Gwendolyn Broward. Although she worked for one of the most famous women in Hollywood, she had never been invited to any of the parties Samara attended.

She walked with Wesley as he strolled about the room greeting the guests.

"The researcher from Los Angeles?" she asked after he'd included that in her introduction.

"It's the truth," he responded.

She and Wesley happened upon a couple of men in heavy discussion.

"I'm plum tired of all the newcomers trying to buy up our land."

The other man looked at Wesley and said, "What do you think?"

"I agree," he responded. "If we sell out all of our property, then pretty soon, nothing will be left. Last year, we were offered a lot of money for our land. They wanted to build a planned community."

"I understand how you all feel," Lydia interjected. "But as an outsider, I can understand why someone would be so taken with Granger's natural beauty."

Dressed like a '20s-era gangster in black pants, black shirt with white suspenders and tie, Wesley looked as handsome as ever. His grandfather was dressed in a similar style but had chosen to sport a fedora hat.

In keeping with the theme, the bar staff served classic cocktail drinks, such as martinis, wine, champagne and mint juleps.

"Did your mother do all of this herself?" Lydia inquired.

"She planned it on her own," Wesley responded. "She even designed the invitation herself."

Adding to the ambiance, light cabaret and jazz music played in the background.

Lydia glanced over at Wesley and said, "You picked out the music, didn't you?"

He laughed. "Guilty."

"Good job," she responded. "I remember that you once mentioned how much you enjoy jazz and some of the early music, so I figured you had a hand in selecting the playlist."

Lydia's eyes traveled to Laney, who was talking to a couple she didn't recognize. Wesley's sister looked lovely in her knee-length, dropped-waist, chiffon dress. Like Lydia, she also wore several long beaded necklaces and red lipstick.

Wesley took her by the hand and led her to a nearby table with seating garnished with red ribbons and baby's breath.

"Are you having a good time?" he asked her. "If not, we can leave."

"No, this is great."

"Everybody loves you."

"No, not everybody, Wes. For one, your

brother thinks I'm a gold digger or something."

"Don't let Jameson get under your skin, sweetheart. I know there is a lot more to you than meets the eye."

She cleared her throat, pretending not to be affected by his words. "I won't," she responded. "I really don't care what he thinks."

Wesley pulled at the collar of his shirt. "I'm ready to get out of this monkey suit."

"I think you look very handsome."

He smiled in response.

The evening was warm. Lydia fanned herself with her hands.

"Would you like to take a walk outside?" Wesley asked. "I don't know about you, but I need to get some air."

"Sure."

Wesley grabbed her gently by the elbow and led her toward the patio doors.

They strolled outside and he took her by the hand.

Lydia closed her eyes, savoring the feel of the night air on her face.

He leaned over and whispered, "I'm really trying hard not to kiss you right now."

Wesley wrapped his arm around her waist.

She glanced up at him. "Then what's stopping you?" Lydia felt the heat of desire wash over her like waves.

Wesley leaned over and kissed her softly on the lips. "I've been wanting to do that all night."

In response, Lydia pulled his head down to hers. Their lips met and she felt buffeted by the winds of a savage harmony. Her senses reeled as if short-circuited, making her knees tremble.

Breaking their kiss, Lydia buried her face against his throat; her trembling limbs clung to him helplessly. She was extremely conscious of where Wesley's warm flesh touched her.

"Why are you so quiet?" he asked after a moment.

"I'm thinking that we just shared a great kiss, and as much as I'd like to do it again, I think that maybe we should head back inside to the party."

"You and Wesley disappeared on us," Maggie commented when her husband and Wesley went to get drinks for them.

"I should've known that you wouldn't miss a thing," Lydia said with a laugh.

"I may not say anything at the time, but I don't miss too much," she acknowledged. Lowering her voice, Maggie added, "Just like I know that you're a woman in love, honey."

Lydia was too stunned to utter a reply.

Am I that obvious? Does it show all over my face? Or when I look at Wes?

Lydia wondered how Wesley would react if he knew the extent of her feelings.

"Oh, dear, I hope I haven't embarrassed you."

"You haven't," Lydia assured Maggie. "You just caught me by surprise. I didn't think my feelings for Wes were so obvious."

"You have the look of a woman in love, Lydia. Wear it with pride." She finished off the last of her martini. "If it makes you feel any better, Wes feels the same way about you. I can tell."

Lydia smiled at Maggie's words, but in the back of her mind, the reality was that Wes had not made such a declaration to her. She was too much of a realist and refused to consider his feelings for other than what he said they were.

"Lydia is a beautiful woman, I'll give her that," Jameson whispered. "I'm just not sure she can be trusted."

"I know how you feel about her, but what you think doesn't matter. The truth is that I'm crazy about Lydia."

Jameson took a sip of his champagne. "I think that much is pretty obvious to everyone around you."

"Maybe not," he responded. "Looks like I might have some competition." Wesley noted the way a few of the male guests were eyeing Lydia. He didn't like how they were looking at the woman he loved.

"You're not jealous, are you?"

"No," Wesley answered. "I just don't think she should be treated like a piece of meat on display."

Jameson laughed. "I never thought I'd live to see the day when you developed a jealous streak."

"I've never cared for another woman in the same way that I care for Lydia. This caught me by complete surprise."

"I didn't realize your feelings were so strong for Lydia."

"I'm falling for her, Jameson. No, I've fallen for her," Wesley corrected.

Their conversation was halted by the appearance of their parents.

Wesley excused himself by saying, "I need to check on my date."

Laney stepped in his path. "Come dance with me."

He glanced over to where Lydia had been standing and found she had disappeared.

"I'm sure she won't mind if you dance with your sister."

"Lead the way," Wes responded.

He was happy to see his sister happy and smiling. Laney looked as if she were having a good time at the party. She looked great; the darkened circles that had been under her eyes were gone.

After they finished dancing, Wesley left his sister in the hands of his grandfather, who was ready to show off his dance skills. Charles's date was sitting at a table with her granddaughter, Patti. He waved to them as he walked off the dance floor.

Lydia smiled when he approached her. "Did I just see you and Laney doing the Charleston? When did you learn it?"

"Would you believe we watched a video?"

"Really?"

Wesley nodded. "I think my sister's been taking lessons or something."

"You both did a great job," she said. "But then, I don't think any of us would really know if you messed up."

He laughed. "I looked for you, but I think you'd stepped outside with Maggie."

"We went to the ladies' room to freshen up," Lydia explained.

He bent down and whispered, "I want you to know that it's pure torture seeing you in this dress. I don't know what it is, but I find you very sexy in this outfit."

"I see," she murmured. "So is this your way of telling me that it turns you on to play dress-up?"

Wesley laughed. "Hmm . . ."

"Don't you go getting any ideas, Wes Broward," she warned. "I'm not about to dress up like a schoolgirl or something kinky like that."

"I was thinking more along the lines of a teacher. You'd look incredible in glasses and your hair pulled back into a bun."

Laughing, she shook her head no. "I don't think so, Wes. Not gonna happen."

He kissed her. "Even if I say pretty please?"

"The answer would still be no."

The look he saw reflected in her eyes mirrored his own.

"Let's get out of here," Wesley stated.

"Where are we going?"

"Somewhere much more private."

CHAPTER 12

Feeling like a giddy teenager, Lydia took Wesley's hand as he led her through the house and down a dimly lit staircase. They were going into the basement, as far as Lydia could tell.

"I can't believe that there's a wine cellar in this house," she said. "It's not something I expected to see. Very nice."

"You will find that we're a pretty eclectic family," Wes responded. "My father and grandfather are collectors of wine."

Despite the cool temperature, Lydia felt flushed. In the darkness, she could still make out Wesley's handsome features.

"So why did you bring me down here?" Lydia asked. "Neither one of us are big wine drinkers."

"I wanted to show you the wine cellar," he responded with a grin. "What are you thinking about?"

She placed a hand to his cheek. "Right

now all I can think about is how much I want you to make love to me."

Wesley covered her mouth with his, kissing her passionately.

Lydia matched him kiss for kiss.

"I really care about you," Wesley whispered as he held her close. "You're all I think about these days."

She smiled. "I feel the same way."

"Are you sure this is what you want?"

"Yes," she murmured.

He kissed her again, his lips traveling to her neck.

Lydia's skin tingled in response as heat radiated from the pit of her stomach. She could not think of anything else — her mind focused solely on what was about to take place.

She was ready to connect with Wesley in this special way. Lydia wanted to give herself completely to him.

Wesley was bursting with desire.

His hand traced a path on her thigh, bringing Lydia's dress upward as he covered her mouth with his own.

She moaned with need, sending a shock wave through his entire body with a savage intensity.

He held her in his arms, making passionate love to her with his gaze. Wesley could hear her uneven breathing as he held her close.

Continuing his slow seduction, Wesley planted kisses on her shoulders, neck and face. As he roused her passion, his own need grew stronger.

He tore at the barrier beneath her dress and quickly removed his own clothing, desperate to feel her skin against his own. For a moment they were poised, locked together, just two people holding each other, heat sizzling between them with only one thing on their minds.

Wesley pulled out a tiny packet, which Lydia knew contained a condom.

He struggled to draw a breath, but Wesley could not do so without inhaling Lydia's fragrance. He felt the fire spreading through every fiber of his being until fervent desire pounded in rhythm with his thundering heart.

Passion pounded the blood through his heart, chest and head, causing Wesley to breathe in deep, soul-drenching drafts. The ever-changing, ever-growing sensations consumed him, mind, body and soul.

They were now committed to one another, branded by their mutual feelings. There was nothing that could destroy their happiness.

■ ■ ■ ■

"Wes, I can't believe we just made love in your family's wine cellar," Lydia murmured as she quickly straightened out her clothes.

"Are you having any regrets?" he asked as he tucked in his shirt.

"No," Lydia said as she pulled a compact out of her purse and combed through her hair with her fingers. "I don't regret what happened between us."

She put away the compact. "Wes, what we just shared was really beautiful. It's just that I've never been so impulsive."

He pulled her into his arms, holding her close. "You make me feel things no other woman has ever made me feel, sweetheart."

"Don't . . ." she said, pulling away from him. "Wes, you don't have to say things that you don't mean just because we . . ."

"I mean every word," he quickly interjected. "Lydia, I'm crazy about you."

She glanced around. "Maybe we should go back to the party, but first, I'd like to freshen up a bit."

"If you walk around that corner there, you'll find a bathroom."

Lydia was relieved to have a moment alone to gather herself. She did not have any regrets about making love to Wesley. She just didn't want him to make any declarations after sex. Her father used to do that whenever he visited. He and her mother would always end up in bed together. He would declare his love, and then the next morning would disappear, leaving Lydia to try to pick up the pieces of her mother's broken heart all over again.

When she came out of the bathroom, it was Wesley's turn.

"I'm going to go back upstairs," she told him.

He kissed her. "Don't disappear on me."

"I won't," Lydia promised.

"Enjoy seeing the wine cellar?" Jameson asked when she walked into the great room.

Startled, Lydia turned around to face him. She hadn't noticed him sitting in one of the wing chairs in the corner. "You nearly scared me to death. I thought I was alone."

He chuckled softly. " 'Fraid not."

She wondered how long Jameson had been in the great room and if he had any idea of what had transpired between her and Wesley in the wine cellar. A wave of embarrassment snaked down Lydia's spine at the thought.

"Did you get a chance to preview any of my father and Grandpa's collection while you were down in the cellar?"

"Yes. Of course," she responded. "That's why we were down there. I have an uncle who is also a collector of wine."

"Really? What's his name?"

"I doubt you've heard of him, but it's Eli Moore." Lydia was telling the truth, but she prayed Jameson would keep his curiosity about her at bay. She really didn't need him searching into her past.

"Are you a wine drinker, Miss . . . I'm sorry, what is your last name?"

She ignored his dig. "Please, just call me Lydia. I drink wine on occasion, but I am not what one could consider a connoisseur by any means. Jameson, what about you?"

He gave a slight smile. "I am not much of a drinker."

They were joined by Wesley a few moments later.

"Jameson, why aren't you at the party?"

"I figured it was time to make my escape. I was actually sitting here trying to decide whether or not to raid the kitchen the way we used to when we were younger."

Wesley laughed. "Jameson and I would always sneak into the kitchen after a party and eat leftovers. I don't know why, but I guess finger sandwiches just aren't our thing."

His brother agreed. "They are certainly not filling."

Wesley glanced over at Jameson and asked, "You in?"

"Yep," he responded. After a moment, he added, "What about you, Lydia? You brave enough to incur the wrath of our cook?"

For the first time since their meeting, Jameson awarded her a warm smile. "Sure, if you two cowboys don't mind having a girl around."

"Make that two girls," Laney interjected from the doorway. "I was never invited to the after-party."

"That's because you were always the one who ratted us out," Jameson declared.

"Well, maybe if you'd invited me, then I never would have said anything, big brother."

Lydia enjoyed the light bantering between Laney and Jameson.

"My brother didn't give you a hard time, did he?" Wesley inquired in a low voice.

"No, it was actually a pleasant conversation," she told him.

They moved into the kitchen.

Jameson walked over to the refrigerator and pulled out containers while Laney grabbed plates for everyone.

Wesley opened a drawer containing eating

utensils.

Lydia's body still tingled from his touch. She felt the hair on the back of her neck stand up, and she glanced over her shoulder. Both Laney and Jameson were watching her.

"What's wrong?" she asked.

"You have something on the back of your head," Laney said. She walked over and removed it. "It looks like part of a wine label. How'd you get that in your hair?"

Lydia flushed in embarrassment.

Laney looked at Wesley.

"I showed her the wine collection," he replied nonchalantly.

Laney broke into a grin but did not say anything.

Lydia heard Jameson snicker and refused to look in his direction. There was no doubt in her mind that he knew exactly what had transpired between her and Wesley. She refused to wilt away in embarrassment, so Lydia held her head up high and said, "That roast looks delicious. I think I'll try that."

Her gaze met Wesley's, and he gave a slight nod of approval.

She sampled the roast and oyster dressing.

Laney pointed to a container sitting in front of her plate. "Lydia, you have to try some of Rusty's chili. People have offered him lots of money for his recipe, but he won't part with it."

"It's been in his family for years," Jameson added. "He won't even cook it when anyone's around. He makes it at his house and brings it over to the main house or the bunkhouse for the cowhands."

"So you don't know what's in it?" Lydia inquired.

"No more than the basics," Wesley said.

She opened the container and spooned some onto her plate. Lydia took several bites and smiled.

"I told you it was delicious," Laney murmured.

They heard a loud grunt and turned to find Rusty standing in the doorway, his arms folded across his chest, a frown on his face. "What you doing in my kitchen?" he demanded. "Making a mess, I see."

"We're going to clean it up," Laney told him with a smile.

"Putting dishes in the dishwasher is not cleaning up."

"Rusty, I love your chili," Lydia told him. A smile trembled to her lips as she added, "It reminds me of my grandmother's chili. She was also very secretive of the ingredients."

He forgot his anger. "Come here, child."

190

Lydia stood up and walked over to Rusty and whispered in his ear.

"You have the recipe?" Laney asked.

She glanced over at Rusty, who nodded.

"Before any of you ask, I am not going to tell. This is a very special recipe, and my grandmother told me that there were only a few people who had it. She made me promise to keep it close to my heart, and I'm going to honor that."

Rusty chuckled at the look of disappointment on the Broward siblings' faces. "I like this woman. She is a keeper, Wes."

"I agree," Wesley responded. "I haven't met many women who could keep a secret."

"Maybe that's because I seem to attract them all," Jameson contributed.

Lydia noticed that Laney had suddenly grown quiet and appeared to be deep in thought. She peered over at Wesley, who was also watching his sister.

A look of worry passed over his handsome features.

"I expect to see my kitchen spotless in the morning," Rusty stated. His tone brooked no argument. "And no dishes in the dishwasher. Clean or no. Dishwasher better be empty."

"We hear you," Jameson assured him.

After they finished eating, Laney said, "I'll

wash the dishes."

"I can help you," Lydia told her.

"Wes, take your date back to the party," Laney ordered gently. "We wouldn't be good hosts if we put you to work."

"I'll stay and help," Jameson offered.

"I'm not in the mood to go back to the party," Wesley told her as they left the kitchen.

"What do you want to do?" Lydia asked.

"Let's go to my house." Wesley stopped walking and took her by the hand. "I need to tell you something."

"What is it?"

"I love you, Lydia."

Her eyes caught and held his. "You're not just saying this to me because of what happened, are you? Do you mean it?"

"I'm saying it because it's the way I really feel about you. *Love* is not a word I toss around casually."

"How did I get to be so lucky?" she wondered aloud.

"The winning bid at the auction for starters," he teased.

"I guess it wasn't a bad way to wrangle you in."

He laughed. "Even if you hadn't bid a penny on me, darlin', I believe we would have ended up in this same place. The moment I laid eyes on you, I was struck by your beauty and the way you carried yourself. I have always desired a woman who was just as beautiful on the inside as on the outside. In a way, we're kindred spirits."

"You really make me feel special, Wes."

"That's because you are," he responded.

Lydia lifted her lips to his.

Wesley kissed her mouth in a tender brushing of his lips that made her smile.

Chapter 13

After saying their goodbyes to his family, Wesley drove Lydia the short distance to his place.

"Alone at last," he murmured in her ear.

Lydia's heart sang with delight. Burying her face against the corded muscles of his chest, she murmured, "What I'm feeling is so extraordinary, it defies description."

Running his fingers through her hair, he asked, "Now, why is that?"

"Because I love you and knowing that you feel the same way . . . I can't explain all of the emotions flowing through me right now." She peered up at him, her eyes wet with unshed tears of joy. "I've never felt so strongly for anyone. It almost scares me, Wes."

"You don't have to be afraid, sweetheart. I will care for your heart in the same way that I care for my own."

Leaning into his embrace, she said,

"Mmm, I like the sound of that."

With one hand, Wesley pulled her closer to him.

Lydia closed her eyes to the feel of his smooth, handsome face against hers. He kissed her, opening her mouth with his.

His kiss sent new spirals of ecstasy through her.

Moving gently down the length of her back, his hands caused Lydia to gasp in sweet agony. She wrapped her arms around him, pulling him close. The feel of his firm, muscled flesh was intoxicating, and Lydia felt the golden wave of love that flowed between them.

Wesley pulled away from her briefly to turn on some music.

He and Lydia held each other tightly as they danced to romantic songs by KEM, Luther Vandross, Brian McKnight and Trey Songz. In the tightness of his embrace, she felt safe and secure.

As Wesley sang to her, an easy smile hovered about her lips.

He stared into her eyes. "I love you so much."

"I love you, too, Wes, with my entire being."

He led her to his bedroom.

Together they savored the warmth of each

other's bodies and the kindling of heated excitement.

As far as Lydia was concerned, they were the only two lovers in the world. Her heart swelled with happiness as Wesley held her tightly and their mouths joined.

In loving him, she had found the peace she had been searching for.

Here in his arms, she would be content forever.

Lydia returned to the hotel shortly after eight the next morning.

Wesley had a busy day scheduled, and she did not want to be in the way. The truth was that she did not want his parents to know that she had spent the night with him. She was worried they might think badly of her.

As she relived the moments of their initial lovemaking in the wine cellar, Lydia questioned, *How could I have been so brazen?*

Lydia felt a renewed surge of embarrassment that Jameson and Laney guessed correctly that they had made love. She had never been one for making love in public places. Wes ignited her desires in such a way that she did things she never would've considered with anyone else.

By declaring their love for one another,

their relationship had reached another pla-
teau.

Her cell phone rang.

Without looking, Lydia knew that it was
Samara.

Releasing a soft sigh, she decided to just
let the call go to voice mail, because at the
moment she wasn't ready to deal with the
real world. Instead, Lydia wanted to stay in
this place of happiness, warmth and love.
She wanted to relish the way it felt when
Wesley held her in his arms. The spirals of
ecstasy she experienced as she gave herself
to him would be forever burned in her
memory.

An hour later, Lydia sat on the sofa with
her laptop, checking emails. She smiled
when she saw one from her best friend, Jasmine. She quickly responded and then
moved on to the next email. The updates to
Samara's website were due to the webmas-
ter, and Lydia had completely forgotten.
This was so not like her.

Lydia opened up a file on her computer
and sorted through it, gathering the information needed. Samara would throw a fit if
her website wasn't updated as she had
requested. She stayed on top of anything
that affected her publicity. The woman was
an expert when it came to self-promotion,

Lydia would give her that.

Having completed the task, she released a long sigh of relief. *I've got to maintain my focus,* she reminded herself. Lydia could not afford to miss any deadlines because Samara would fire her in a heartbeat.

She glanced over at the phone. It was time she checked in with the boss lady.

Wesley was in his office when Lydia arrived with lunch.

When they spoke earlier, he had mentioned his craving for Mexican food, so she stopped and picked up some to surprise him.

He was on the telephone and gestured for her to take a seat.

"Hey, I'm glad you received my message," Wesley said into the receiver. "I've made a decision. I'm accepting the offer for the land in Hastings."

He glanced at her and winked.

"Yeah, it is a very generous offer. Well over what I was selling the place for," he said. "Really? That's good to hear."

"You've decided to sell some of your land?" she asked when Wesley ended the call.

He nodded. "It's actually a ranch. I thought about what you said, and this is what I want to do. The buyer is a rancher from Texas. I'm glad it will go to someone who will appreciate its history and everything it has to offer."

"Congratulations," Lydia said. "We have to celebrate."

Wesley met her gaze. "What do you have in mind?"

"For starters, I brought Mexican," she responded, holding up the bag. "After that, we will just have to play it by ear."

He smiled. "I didn't expect you to go out and get the food when I mentioned it earlier, but thank you, Lydia. It's much appreciated."

"I wanted to do it for you, Wes."

They left the office and went into the dining room.

Lydia placed a plate in front of Wesley. "The girl at the restaurant said that it was your favorite. I guess you must eat there a lot, or she knows you on a personal level."

He laughed. "It's the only Mexican restaurant in Granger."

She shrugged. "Hey, I'm just saying . . ." she said. "I'm curious, Wes. Why did you want to sell that ranch?"

"I bought it with the original idea to make it a BWB II, but then I started feeling restless and wasn't sure what I wanted to do with it. I just figured it would be best to sell it to someone who had the time and dedication to develop it into a working ranch once more."

"So you don't have any real ties to it?" she asked.

"Not really," Wesley answered. "I bought it after the owner died. His family was deep in debt and would've lost everything."

"I'm sure you purchased it for more than it was worth."

"Now I've made my money back and more," he told her.

Lydia and Wesley cleaned up after they ate.

"Do you have to go back into town?" he asked.

"No, not really. Why?"

"I thought maybe we could spend the rest of the day together. We can take the horses and ride to the lake."

"Are you planning on getting into the water?" Lydia asked. "I didn't bring a swimsuit with me."

"I bought you one," Wesley announced. "I figured you'd be spending a lot more time here, and I love to swim. I hope you don't mind my being so presumptuous."

She reached up and pulled his face down to hers.

■ ■ ■ ■

The ringing of a phone chased Lydia out of a peaceful sleep.

She groaned as she fumbled around the nightstand for her cell phone. Her fingers grasped it, inadvertently hitting the accept button. Lydia could hear Samara's voice even before she put it to her ear.

"I've been trying to reach you since last night. Why haven't you answered your phone?"

"Because I've been busy, Samara," Lydia responded. She eased out of bed and checked the bathroom.

Wesley was not there.

Her eyes strayed to the clock. He had probably been gone for hours.

"You wanted me to spend more time with Wes, and I've been doing just that." Lydia did not mention that she was at his house. Samara had no idea that she and Wesley were involved, and she saw no need to tell her. She was entitled to a personal life, Lydia reasoned.

"That's good to hear."

"I didn't answer the phone last night because I didn't want to make him suspicious," she stated. "When we spoke yesterday, I told you that I'd give you a call this evening."

"The reason I've been calling you is because I have some great news. I've cleared my schedule and I want to come to Granger. I need you to make the necessary arrangements."

"You're doing what?" Lydia asked.

"I'm coming to Granger. I'm really looking forward to meeting Wesley Broward and his family."

None of this was making any sense to Lydia. She still had no real idea why Samara was so interested in the Broward family. But why had she suddenly decided to come to Granger? Another question came to mind: Was she interested in Wes?

"When do you plan to arrive?" she asked after finding her voice.

"Book a private plane for me for the day after tomorrow. My publicist has already been in contact with the media."

"So you want everyone to know that you're going to be in town, then." It was a statement and not a question. Whom she worked for would no longer be a secret.

"Of course," Samara stated matter-of-factly.

"I guess I need to get busy then," Lydia stated. "I'll give you a call later with all of the details, Samara."

"Make sure that you do."

Lydia ended the call just as Wesley walked into the bedroom. She pasted on a smile.

"I just came by to see if you were up," he told her.

She stood up. "I'm up."

He eyed her for a moment. "Honey, are you okay?"

She nodded. "I'm fine."

"From that expression on your face, I would have to believe otherwise."

Lydia decided to be honest. "Wes, the woman I work for is Samara Lionne."

His eyebrow raised a fraction. "Really?"

She nodded. "The reason I'm telling you now is because she's coming to Granger."

"You are Samara's assistant?"

"Yeah."

"I'm impressed."

"That's good because she wants to meet you, Wes," Lydia announced. The thought of Samara's desire to meet him really bothered her. Mostly because she had no idea what her boss was really up to.

"You seem distracted," Wesley said, cutting into her thoughts. "Does it bother you that much that Samara is coming to town?"

"She can be a bit irritating at times," Lydia confessed.

"I can believe that," he responded. "She strikes me as a bit of a diva."

"With a capital *D*." She chuckled. "I probably shouldn't have said that about the woman who signs my paychecks."

"You won't have to deal with her alone, sweetheart. We can introduce her to Jameson. Who knows? It might be a match made in heaven. He can relax because she won't be after his money."

"Wes, I like your brother."

He threw back his head and laughed.

"I can't believe that you never mentioned that you worked with Samara Lionne. She is my favorite actress of all time," Maggie stated. "I'm so excited that she's coming to town."

She had come to visit with Lydia while her husband was attending a meeting in one of the conference rooms downstairs.

"I'm sorry but I couldn't tell anyone. Wes didn't even know until now." Lydia was anything but excited about Samara's visit. She hoped that it would be only for a few days and that Samara wasn't going to demand her return to Los Angeles. Lydia did not want to leave Wesley, although they had discussed his coming to L.A. with her. Still, she wasn't ready to leave Granger. She had fallen in love with the small town.

"I hope that you'll introduce us."

"Sure."

"Hey, what's wrong with you, sugar?"

"Maggie, I'm not looking forward to Samara's visit," Lydia confessed. "I actually like things the way they are."

Her friend nodded. "You think she'll try and come between you and Wes?"

Lydia shrugged. "I really don't know what to expect. Samara's been very secretive about her plans. Maybe I'm overreacting."

"I'm pretty sure that you don't have anything to worry about," Maggie reassured her. "Wes is crazy about you, Lydia."

"It's not that I'm worried about Samara and Wes. I would just feel a lot better if I knew the reason for her trip to Granger. If she had planned on coming here in the first place, then why send me?"

"Well, from what I hear, some celebrities can be quite fickle at times," Maggie responded.

"Working with Samara will give me the experience I need for what I'd like to do in the future."

"You want to be an actress?" Maggie inquired.

Lydia shook her head no. "I would rather manage talent," she said.

"Well, look at you . . ."

"It's what I've always dreamed of doing."

"I think you'd be good at something like that, for sure, but how does Wes fit into those plans?"

She met Maggie's gaze. "He is very supportive of my dreams."

"Well, there you have it, Lydia. Proof positive that Wes is the man for you." Maggie leaned forward and said, "Now, I'm gonna tell you the truth. Wesley Broward has the makings of a wonderful husband. Don't you go letting him slip through your fingers like water. Somebody will be there to catch him." She rose to her expensively clad feet. "I've said my piece, so I'm going to find Dane and have a nice lunch."

The two women embraced.

"Thanks for the visit and the girl talk," Lydia told her.

When Maggie left, she went back to her work — making arrangements for Samara's visit.

She tried to ignore the deep sense of foreboding, but it was to no avail. Lydia tried to reassure herself that nothing could go wrong. But she couldn't help but wonder how Samara was going to react when she found out about her relationship with Wesley.

Lydia told herself that it wouldn't matter unless Samara had designs on the man for herself. She would just have to make it clear that Wesley was already taken.

CHAPTER 14

Lydia watched from the sidelines as Samara's arrival was treated as a major town event. Media and townspeople alike flanked the small airport. There was even a camera crew from a Helena TV station filming.

Samara's publicist had called earlier with the date and time of the actress's interview on a local morning show in Granger.

She met Samara at the waiting limo. "How was your flight?"

"It's wasn't bad at all. The food wasn't that great though." Samara admired her manicured nails. "Where did you put me? I hope it's a five-star hotel."

"Granger doesn't have a five-star hotel," Lydia quickly interjected. "It only has one hotel — the same one I'm staying in and it's nice enough I booked you the suite next to mine."

"Oh, well, I guess that will have to do."

Lydia rolled her eyes heavenward. Samara

could be a little too much to take at times. She consoled herself with the fact that babysitting her boss for a few days wouldn't be too bad. Samara would have to return to Los Angeles for work, including her role in the upcoming cowboy film.

It was strange that she had not heard anything about this project. Lydia had not seen it mentioned in *Variety* or any other entertainment magazine. Apparently, they were keeping it very hush-hush. Lydia made a mental note to ask Samara about it.

"Where are we having dinner?" Samara asked. "I'm in the mood for seafood."

"It's almost noon and you're already thinking about dinner."

Samara gave her a rare smile. "Dinner is my favorite meal of the day. I take it very seriously."

Lydia chuckled. She liked this side of Samara, although she rarely saw it.

Wesley called her minutes after she arrived back at the hotel.

"How are things going?" he asked.

"Well," she responded. "But I'm going to have to stay here this evening. Samara and I are having dinner together."

"I understand," Wesley told her. "I'll miss seeing you, but I will try to manage being away from you one night."

She laughed. "I'm sure you'll be fine."

Samara managed to keep her busy until it was time for them to leave for the restaurant.

"This is a pretty little town," Samara said as she glanced over the menu. "I like the tranquility."

Lydia agreed.

"What have you been doing in this town besides getting to know Wesley Broward?" Samara inquired. "Is there anything to do for recreation?"

"There's a lot to do," Lydia explained. "There's always a festival of some sort going on. There's horseback riding, picnics on the lake . . . Helena's only a hundred miles away if you're looking for more of a city nightlife."

"You look well rested," Samara stated as she surveyed Lydia.

"I've enjoyed my time here in Granger."

"I'm glad to hear it." Samara glanced around the restaurant. "I have a feeling I'm going to like it here, as well."

"I haven't heard anything about your new movie yet," Lydia stated.

Samara waved her hand in dismissal. "It's still pretty early on. I don't want to talk about work. Tell me about Wesley. When do I get to meet him?"

"There's really nothing more to tell you about him," Lydia responded. "As for meeting him, I'll have to check his schedule. He's a very busy man."

"He's not too busy for you, I'm sure."

Lydia picked up her glass of tea and took a long sip to control her temper.

"I normally don't get excited about interviews, but I have to tell you, Lydia. I'm really jazzed about this one tomorrow."

"Why is that?"

Samara shrugged. "I don't know."

Lydia felt quite the opposite. She did not relish the idea of Samara being in Granger, but there was nothing she could do about it. She would probably feel a lot better if she knew what her boss was really up to, perhaps. Lydia had worked with Samara long enough to know that she did not just impulsively decide to come to Granger.

"Hellooo . . ."

"Oh, I'm sorry," Lydia muttered. "Were you saying something?"

"No, thank goodness. You wouldn't have heard a word of it." Samara leaned back in her chair. "Why are you so preoccupied?"

"I'm not," Lydia responded. "I was just thinking about tomorrow and everything that has to be done."

"Everything is working according to plan.

Just relax and enjoy the evening."

"What plan?"

"My plan," Samara responded. "That's all that you need to know."

Her words made Lydia feel uneasy. Samara was definitely up to something, but she had no idea what it could be.

"I miss you," Wesley said when she answered the phone. He and Jameson had taken an evening ride, but he still felt restless.

She smiled. "I miss you, too."

"Where's your boss?"

"Samara just retired to her room for the evening."

"Why don't you come out here?" Wesley suggested. "Or I could come to the hotel. I don't think I can sleep without you next to me."

"I would, but we have to be at the TV station early tomorrow morning for an interview. I think it's best that I just get some sleep. I have a feeling it's going to be a long day tomorrow."

"Are you saying that we won't get any sleep if we're together?" Wesley inquired.

Lydia laughed. "You know that we won't."

He knew that she was right. Wesley couldn't seem to get enough of her. The more they made love, the more he hungered for her. "Well, can I at least have a good-night kiss?"

"How do you plan to accomplish this?"

"Open your door."

She gasped. "You're here at the hotel?"

Lydia jumped up and rushed to the door, throwing it open.

"You've spoiled me. I need you by my side."

Dropping the phone, she hugged him. "I'm so glad that you're here."

"I thought you said . . ."

Lydia cut him off by saying, "Shut up and kiss me."

Wesley traced his fingertip across her lip, causing her skin to tingle when he touched her. He paused to kiss Lydia, sending currents of desire through her.

"Make love to me," she whispered between kisses. Lydia no longer cared that Samara was just down the hall.

"You don't know how badly I wanted to hear those words come out of your mouth," he confessed. "My body yearns for yours."

Wesley bent his head and captured her lips in a demanding kiss.

Locking her hands behind his neck, Lydia returned his kiss, matching passion for passion.

He helped her undress. His breath seemed to catch when he glimpsed her in her underwear.

"You are so beautiful," Wesley said, his voice filled with a reverent awe.

He undressed and then joined her in bed. Wesley's mouth covered hers again hungrily.

Lydia answered his kiss with a desire that belied her outward calm.

Moaning, she drew herself closer to Wesley as his hands explored her body. He moved his mouth down the column of her neck, teasing with his lips against her sensitive skin. Lydia fought a shiver as his mouth found her collarbone.

Lydia marveled at the way Wesley made her feel. The way their bodies connected and became one in a fluid motion. Nothing had ever felt this perfect. Or so right.

She loved him with her whole heart.

And then she loved him some more.

Lydia matched her breaths to his until they both were breathing in a normal rhythm.

"We are perfect together," she murmured, as Wesley settled next to her, with one arm thrown over her body in a protective gesture.

"I was actually thinking along the lines of earth-shattering."

CHAPTER 15

"I have to head out to the ranch, but I'll give you a call later," Wesley announced as he got dressed.

She ran her fingers through her curls. "I can't wait for this interview to be over. Maybe I'll find out how much longer Samara plans to be in town. She's been pretty vague each time I've asked."

"Do you think that maybe she wants to have the movie filmed in Granger?"

Lydia hadn't considered that possibility. "That could be it," she responded. Maybe she wanted to use the BWB Ranch as the setting. This would certainly explain her interest in the Broward family.

He kissed her. "I have to get going. I love you."

"I love you, too."

An hour later, she and Samara walked out of the hotel and got into a limo.

"How did you sleep?" Lydia inquired.

"Quite well, actually." Samara glanced over at her and asked, "What about you? You weren't up most of the night working, were you?"

"No," Lydia responded with a secret smile. "I went to bed shortly after I left your room."

They were directed to the greenroom as soon as they arrived at the television station. Lydia took a seat on the black leather sofa while Samara was having her hair and makeup done.

She did not feel as antsy as she had in the beginning. Lydia decided that she had overreacted where Samara was concerned.

Her eyes traveled to the clock on the wall. It was almost time for the actress to go on the set. She got up to make sure Samara was ready.

Watching from the greenroom, Lydia admired the way Samara handled herself during the interview. She talked about her current movie role.

"I loved playing Jaden," she was saying. "I enjoy playing strong women."

"So tell us, what brings you to Granger?" the host inquired.

"My interest was piqued when I read about the town in a travel magazine," she admitted. "But I fell in love the moment I stepped off the plane and glimpsed the mountains, the trees, fresh air and the town itself. It's so beautiful here."

Lydia could understand because she felt the same way.

"We are thrilled to have you visit with us. How long will you be staying?"

"I'm actually planning to move to Granger," Samara announced with a grin. "I've already found a lovely ranch outside of town that's absolutely magical. Of course, there are a lot of renovations that have to be completed, and when they're finished the place will be perfect."

Lydia gasped in surprise.

When did Samara decide this? she wondered.

"I knew the moment my real estate agent emailed me the photos that this was the perfect place for me to live and raise a family. It reminds me of the house I grew up in," Samara stated. "Although it was much smaller."

"Are you thinking of settling down?"

Samara smiled. "I am," she confirmed. "Although I'm still looking for Mr. Wonderful. I wanted to find a place that would be my retreat from the rest of the world. I also wanted a place for my future children to have that experience to play outside . . . run with the dogs . . . whatever."

What in the world was Samara really up to? Why had she been so secretive about her plans to move to Granger? Lydia felt that initial wave of apprehension wash over her. She had no idea what was going on with her boss, and it made her extremely nervous.

"Granger's very lucky to have you as a resident."

"Thank you," Samara murmured. "Once all of the renovations are completed, I'd be more than happy to give you a tour."

"Samara, exactly when did you decide you were moving to Granger?" Lydia demanded once the camera stopped rolling and they were in the greenroom. "You told me that this was about a movie role. I'd like to know what's really going on here."

"We're not going to have this discussion right now," Samara stated coolly. "Why don't you take me to meet Wesley Broward? Don't you think it's time he and I met?"

"Why do you want to meet him?" Lydia asked, her arms folded across her chest. She did not like the direction in which they were headed. A part of her wondered if Samara was interested in Wesley. It was the only thing that really made sense to her.

Samara eyed her for a moment before saying, "You're acting very protective of this man. Is there something I should know?"

"Wes and I are seeing each other," Lydia announced after a brief pause. "We have grown really close, and I really care about him."

"That's so sweet," Samara cooed. "Honey, you don't have to be jealous of me — I assure you that I'm not interested in Wesley romantically."

"You're also not here to prepare for a movie, so what is really going on?" Lydia wanted to know. "I don't understand all of the lies. I deserve to know why you really had me come to Montana."

"Instead of asking all these questions, you really should be thanking me, Lydia. After all, you never would've met Wesley Broward if not for the assignment I gave you." She folded her arms across her chest. "You're welcome."

Lydia was not satisfied with Samara's lack of response to her questions. "You're going to have to come clean, Samara. I'm not going to take you to meet Wes until you tell me the truth."

"I can't tell you anything right now, but I promise that you'll understand everything really soon. I need you to trust me on this, Lydia."

Samara was not budging, so they were at

a standstill.

"Fine," Lydia responded, but deep down she felt anything but fine.

She called Wesley and asked, "Do you have some time to join us for lunch?"

"Sure," he responded smoothly. "When and where?"

"Las Margaritas around noon," Lydia murmured. "Samara loves Mexican food."

"I'll see you there."

"I had no idea when I sent you here that you would manage to fall in love with Wesley Broward. Imagine that. Maybe I should become a matchmaker."

Lydia did not utter a response.

Although Samara said that she wasn't interested in Wesley romantically, Lydia wasn't sure that she believed her. Especially from the way the woman was fawning over him. She seemed to be working awfully hard to garner his interest. They had not been seated more than five minutes when she started coming on to him.

Boss or no boss, Samara had no right to blatantly flirt with the man involved with Lydia.

"I've been told that all of the Broward men are charming," Samara said with a smile. "I haven't met the rest of your family, but they were certainly right about you."

"Why, thank you, ma'am," Wesley uttered.

Lydia bit back a chuckle at the expression on Samara's face. She definitely did not like Wesley referring to her as *ma'am*.

Samara sent her a sharp look, but Lydia did not care. The self-absorbed actress was making a play for her man.

She boldly met Samara's gaze.

Lightly fingering a lamp on a nearby table, Samara said, "Lydia's told me so much about the BWB Ranch that I'm dying to see it for myself."

"It would be an honor to have you visit," Wesley said, his tone polite and formal.

"I can't wait."

Lydia stole a peek at Wesley. He appeared to be studying Samara. She was relieved to see that he was not buying her act completely.

They made small talk while they ate.

When Wesley signaled for the check, Samara told him, "No, this is on me. Please don't refuse me."

He would not hear of it. "I will take care of payment."

"Is today a good day for that tour?" Samara inquired. She flashed him a sexy grin.

"Wes is a very busy man," Lydia quickly interjected. "I don't think we need to take up any more of his time."

"You're right, Lydia. We should let him get back to what he does best — ranching."

"It's real nice to meet you, Miss Lionne. How long will you be staying in town?" Wesley inquired. "I want to make sure we get you out to the ranch."

"Don't you worry about that," Samara said smoothly. "We have plenty of time."

Confused, Wesley glanced over at Lydia.

"Oh, I'm not in Granger for a visit. I'm moving here. Well, just outside of town."

Lydia met his gaze. "I just found out this morning."

"Wesley, I bought a lovely little property in Hastings," Samara announced. "I think it was called the Hastings Dude Ranch. I'm changing the name, of course." She clasped her hands together in glee. "I can't wait to start the renovations. This is going to be so much fun."

"The Hastings property," Wes repeated slowly. He looked from Samara to Lydia in disbelief. "Please tell me that you had nothing to do with this."

Bewildered, Lydia shook her head. "No, I had no idea about any of her plans." She glanced over at Samara and then back at Wesley. "I found out about this just now. She mentioned earlier that she found a place, but she didn't say anything about the name or location. Wes, I was kept in the dark about this."

"The place is perfect for what I have in mind," Samara continued to gush, seemingly oblivious to Wesley's anger.

"I own that property," Wesley uttered. His eyes grew cold as he stared at Lydia accusingly. He had told her about his plan to sell it. She had to have mentioned it to Samara. She was the only one outside of his family who knew of his desire.

"You *did* own it," Samara corrected. "I own it now. What a coincidence. I think it must be fate."

Wesley glared at Lydia. "I find it hard to believe that you had no idea what was going on, especially since you were there when I decided to sell."

"Wes, I assure you that I had nothing to do with Samara buying that property," Lydia stated. "Believe it or not, Samara does not fill me in on all of her plans."

"So why did you really come here?" he demanded. "Were you really doing research for a movie role?"

Lydia glanced over at Samara. "I don't know the real answer to that question, I'm afraid."

"She came here because I told her to,"

Samara interjected. "That's all you need to know, Mr. Broward."

"Now, see, that's where you're wrong," he responded angrily. "You bought that ranch under false pretenses. It was a fraudulent transaction."

"I merely disguised my identity from the seller," she said with a shrug. "I didn't want it publicized that I was buying property here. That's all."

"Wes . . ."

He glared at Lydia. "Jameson said that you were trouble. Maybe I should have listened to him."

"Excuse me," she responded. "Your brother doesn't know me well enough to have any opinion."

Her eyes flashed in her anger. "I can't believe you, Wes. You of all people should know that I wouldn't do something like this."

He shook his head. "I don't know what to believe."

Before she could say anything, he stalked off, walking briskly toward his car.

Lydia was stunned. She wasn't sure what had just happened. Everything had been going so well. But now . . .

Samara was unfazed. She chattered nonstop it seemed during the ride back to the hotel.

"What is your problem?" Samara demanded when she realized that Lydia had not said a word to her.

Her temper flared and Lydia did not bother to disguise her feelings. "I don't have any idea what you're up to, but I don't want to be a part of it."

"It's too late, don't you think?" Samara asked. "You became a part of my plan the moment you set foot in Granger." She paused a heartbeat before adding, "Lydia, don't you worry about Wesley Broward. Mark my words . . . that cowboy of yours will come to his senses and will be knocking on your door. Just wait and see."

She glowered at her and turned away. Lydia was breathless with rage.

"In the meantime, there is a lot to be done to prepare the Hastings property. You're going to be so busy, you won't have time to think about the man. Oh, I'm giving you a big, fat bonus. Is this great news?"

Lydia continued her silence.

"Did you hear me?"

"I heard you, Samara, and you know something — I really don't care." Rancor sharpened her voice. "You can keep your bonus."

"You can't be serious."

"Oh, I'm very serious," Lydia responded, flashing Samara a look of disdain.

They did not speak during the rest of ride back to the hotel.

Lydia jumped out with the intent to head straight to her room.

Samara caught up with her at the elevators.

"When we get upstairs, I need you to —"

Lydia cut her off by saying, "I'm going to my room, and I don't want to be disturbed."

Samara paled. "Excuse me?"

"I mean it," she uttered. "I've had enough of you for one day."

"I know you're upset over this cowboy, but if Wesley Broward cares for you, he will be back, Lydia."

"I'm not having this conversation with you of all people." Her voice was quiet yet held an undertone of cold contempt.

"I really don't care much for your tone, Lydia. Apparently, you've clearly forgotten who you are working for."

"Trust me, I haven't forgotten, Samara."

They rode the elevator in tense silence.

When the doors opened, Lydia stepped out first.

Samara caught up with her. "Look, I know that you're upset over the way I handled this situation, but don't say something you might regret."

"I'm going to my room, and I'll see you tomorrow."

Samara blocked her path. "Lydia, I'm not done. I need to go over what I want for dinner."

"I'm afraid you are going to have to make the call yourself," Lydia stated as she made her way to the door. "I mean it. I'm not doing anything else for you. I just need to be alone."

"I can't believe you're being so silly where Wesley's concerned."

"I really care about him," Lydia stated, turning around to face Samara.

"And if he truly cares about you, he won't let me come between you two."

Lydia quickly unlocked her door. She needed to get as far away from Samara as possible. When she first landed the job as her assistant, Lydia could not have been more pleased. But now . . . she was so angry that she could spit nails.

Wesley was furious with himself.

He could not believe that he had freely given his heart to Lydia — a woman he knew nothing about. Jameson had said all along that she could not be trusted, and clearly he was right.

She had been lying to him all along.

"What's wrong with you?" Jameson asked. "You've been in a bad mood since you came back from town."

"It's nothing I want to talk about," he muttered.

"Have you met Samara Lionne, the woman Lydia works for?"

"Yeah," Wesley growled. "She's nothing like the woman I thought she would be."

"Did something happen?"

"Samara bought my property in Hastings," he announced. "I never intended to sell it to some stuck-up actress."

"I suppose Lydia had a hand in this," Jameson said.

Wesley nodded. "She says that she didn't, but I told her about the ranch. I really thought she could be trusted."

"I'm sorry, bro."

"Lesson learned," he uttered with a shrug.

CHAPTER 16

The next morning, Lydia's sorrow had been replaced by anger. She was furious with Samara for her deception and angry with Wesley for his distrust. Mostly, she was mad at herself for getting in the middle of this mess.

Lydia opened her suitcase and began packing. She didn't care how much money Samara was paying her — this job had already cost her too much. It wasn't just the loss of Wesley, but the loss of her dignity.

She made arrangements to drop her rental car off at the airport.

There's one more thing I need to do before I leave.

Lydia left her room and walked two doors down to where Samara was staying.

"You're late," she uttered when Lydia walked into her hotel room. Looking her from head to toe, Samara questioned, "Why are you dressed like that? I have an interview in Helena and we need to leave in about five minutes."

"I quit," Lydia announced. "Don't worry, there's a car waiting downstairs to drive you to Helena and back."

"Excuse me?"

"I no longer work for you."

Samara's eyes flashed in her anger. "I'm sorry . . . am I being punked?"

She glanced around the room. "Where are the cameras? I know this is not happening to me right now. *It can't be.*"

"I appreciate the opportunity to work for you, but I can't do this anymore."

"Do what?" Samara demanded. "Make a lot of money."

"I am not willing to sell my soul for any amount," Lydia replied. "I'm sorry, but I quit and I'm going back to Los Angeles."

"You won't be able to get a job in the entertainment industry — I'll make sure of it."

"Samara, I'm really not worried about you. The tabloids could have a field day with everything I know."

"You wouldn't dare."

"You're right, Samara. I'm nothing like you, so I won't stoop to your level."

"Get out of here."

Lydia broke into a smile. "Gladly."

A string of curses followed her as she left

Samara's room and returned to her own. Lydia realized that this was what she should've done months ago. She should have trusted her instincts.

Then I never would've met Wesley.

And I wouldn't be walking around with a broken heart, she added silently.

The knock on the door cut into her somber thoughts.

When she opened the door, Wesley brushed past her. "We need to talk."

He saw her suitcases in the middle of the floor. "What's going on? Are you leaving?"

Lydia nodded.

He stepped around the luggage. "I guess I shouldn't be surprised."

Her arms folded across her chest, Lydia asked, "What do you mean by that?"

"Apparently that's what you do when you've been found out," Wesley stated. "You run away."

"Wes, let's get something straight," Lydia responded coolly. "I'm not running away from you or anything else. The reason I'm leaving is because I quit my job and there is nothing left in Granger for me."

"I see."

"Why are you here, Wes?"

"I want you to tell me to my face why you lied to me," he responded.

"I didn't lie to you, but you would rather believe the worst of me, apparently."

"I don't know what else to think."

"How about considering the truth of this situation?" Lydia asked. "The truth, Wes, is that I had no idea that Samara was looking to purchase property in Montana. She never once mentioned it."

"You and I discussed that exact piece of property that she bought. How do you explain this?"

"I don't know," Lydia responded. "It has to be a coincidence."

Wesley shook his head. "Sorry, I'm not buying that."

"I don't know what you want me to say. I've been honest with you, Wes."

"I had this vision of moving to L.A. with you, traveling with you or doing both, Lydia. I guess I thought we were a team. Apparently, it was you and Samara who were on the same team."

His words hurt her to the core.

"We have nothing else to say to one another if you believe that, Wes."

"I thought that selling that property was a testament to how much I wanted to start a life with you. Instead, you only viewed it as an opportunity for your boss."

"I think it's best that you leave now,"

Lydia stated. "I don't want to be in the same room with a man who doesn't trust me." She blinked back tears. "I don't want to be in the same town. You talk about honesty, but you lied to me, as well."

"What are you talking about?" he asked with a frown on his face.

"You lied when you said that you loved me," Lydia told him.

"Are you saying that you don't believe that I love you?" Wesley questioned. "What have I done to cause you to doubt me?"

"I can't overlook the fact that you immediately thought the worst of me when Samara made her announcement. A man who really loves a woman wouldn't jump to that type of conclusion."

"You lied to me from the very beginning, Lydia. We were able to get past that because you decided to tell me the truth. I came here this morning because I'm willing to forget about everything that's happened," Wesley responded. "The truth is that I *was* looking to sell the place. I preferred not to sell it to some actress though."

She fumed. "You still don't get it, do you? Wes, the only thing I am guilty of is falling in love with the wrong man. Now, if you will excuse me, I have a plane to catch."

"Lydia, I don't want you to leave." He

reached for her.

She retreated backward. "Wesley, I have to do what is right for me, and being here in Granger . . . It's not where I need to be."

"You seem a little preoccupied," Steven told his son. "Is everything okay?"

"I found out earlier that I sold the Hastings Ranch to Samara Lionne," Wesley announced. "I was misled into believing that I was selling to a rancher in Texas. I told Lydia about the property, and now it's conveniently owned by the same woman she works for."

"I see," his father uttered.

"I'm in love with Lydia."

"Now, that doesn't come as news to me, son. I saw that coming the night she paid ten thousand dollars for a date with you."

"Lydia wants me to believe that she didn't have anything to do with Samara's plan to buy the ranch." He gave a slight shrug. "I don't know what to believe."

"Sometimes the things that first bring a couple together ain't necessarily the thing that will keep them together," his father stated. "This turn of events will do one of two things. You two will be stronger for it, or you will find that ending the relationship is the best for the both of you. For example, your mother may not have been my first choice for a bride, but after thirty-four wonderful years, I have to say that she was the best choice for me."

"I love Lydia in every sense of the word."

"Use this time apart to really think about what it is you really want, son," Steven advised. "Be sure before you make your next move."

Wesley considered his father's words.

He had gone over to the hotel with the intent to work things out with Lydia. Wesley was surprised to find that she was heading back to Los Angeles. Her work here was done, he reasoned sadly.

Deep down he wanted to believe that his assumptions were wrong, but there was too much evidence against her. Regardless, he loved her and was ready to forgive Lydia. However, she had no interest in their relationship. She wanted to put as much distance between her and Granger as possible.

Had their entire relationship been a lie?

The question nagged at Wesley.

Lydia entered her apartment and set her luggage in a corner. She wiped a tear from her cheek.

During the plane ride back to Los Angeles, she spent a lot of time thinking about her recent decisions. Was she too hasty in quitting her job? Would Samara really have her blacklisted?

She tried to avoid the one question that kept popping up. Did she do the right thing by leaving Granger? By leaving Wesley behind?

I had to leave, Lydia reasoned silently. *I needed to put some distance between myself and Wes. I don't know why I ever thought we could ride off into the sunset together.*

"Real life is nothing like that," she uttered. Lydia felt an instant's squeezing hurt.

Overcome with pent-up emotion, she slumped to the floor in sobs.

She loved him so much.

When she was all cried out, Lydia forced herself up off the floor and into the bathroom.

She felt a little better after her shower.

Lydia was tired and emotionally spent. She hadn't slept well because she couldn't stop thinking about Wesley. She sat on the edge of her bed with a towel wrapped around her.

I'll survive this, Lydia kept telling herself. *I will get through this heartache.*

It helped to have those thoughts, but deep down, she knew that she would never love another man the way that she loved Wesley.

Perhaps it was for the best, Lydia reasoned. She had lost herself in him by loving so deeply. She did not want to ever love that way again — it hurt too much when the relationship ended.

This is the way my mother loved my father, Lydia realized. Why she could never just close her heart to him.

She refused to let that happen to her. What she had with Wesley was over. Lydia had to find the strength to move forward with her life and her dreams. It was the only way she could provide for her mom. She didn't want her mother to continue working those long hours.

Wesley dropped down beside his sister. They were at the pool at the main house. "I've been worried about you, Laney."

"You don't have to be," she responded without looking at him. "I'm fine, Wes."

"No, you're not," he countered. "I know when my sister is going through something."

Laney changed the subject by asking, "Where is Lydia?"

"Probably back in Los Angeles by now," Wesley stated.

She was surprised by his response. "She left town?"

He nodded.

"I thought she worked for Samara Lionne," Laney said. "Isn't she in Granger?"

Wesley wasn't going to unburden himself on his sister, especially since she was dealing with something on her own.

He wrapped an arm around her. "Laney, I want you to know that if you need anything, I'm here for you."

She smiled. "I know that, Wes."

"You can tell me anything."

"I love you," Laney told him. "But there are some things that I have to work out for myself. This is one of those times."

They embraced.

"Wes, why did Lydia leave? It looked to me like you two were getting really close."

"I guess she decided that it was for the best."

He should have known that Laney was not going to just let it go at that. "Did you two have a fight?"

"It's one of those things that will have to work itself out, Laney."

She rose up, saying, "I like Lydia. You two are good for one another."

"Have you seen Laney?" his mother asked a few minutes later. "I thought Rusty said that she was at the pool."

"She just left here to go to her own place." Wesley removed his shirt. Maybe a swim would help to clear his head.

"How did she seem to you?"

"Okay," Wesley responded. "She'll be fine, Mama. Laney's just working through something, and she obviously doesn't want our help."

Gwendolyn sat down beside him and announced, "I watched the morning show this morning."

"I didn't see it, but I met Samara Lionne," Wesley stated. "She's interesting."

"I was about to say the same thing."

"I already told Dad, so you might as well know. She bought my property in Hastings," Wesley announced. "If I'd known the identity of the buyer, I never would've sold it to her. She told me that she's having it renovated. It doesn't sound like she wants a working ranch."

His mother appeared thoughtful for a moment. "Do you think that Lydia had anything to do with this?"

"How else would she have known about the property?"

Gwendolyn shook her head. "Somehow I can't see Lydia doing something like this to you, Wes. That young woman really cares for you."

"Mama, I'm not sure I can ever trust her again."

"Have you discussed this with her?"

"She denied it, of course."

"Lydia could be telling the truth, Wes. Things are not always the way they appear."

CHAPTER 17

"Lydia, I'm so glad that you're back!" Jasmine exclaimed. "I really missed you. When did you get in?"

"Yesterday," she responded as she hugged her best friend. "I came home and went straight to bed. I was really tired." Lydia decided she needed to get out of her apartment for a little while. She did not intend to stay home and mope around over a man who didn't deserve her. Instead, she called her best friend and invited her to lunch.

They sat down in a booth near the window of the café.

After they placed their drink and food orders, Jasmine said, "The last time I spoke with you, Samara was flying to Granger. I told you that woman was high maintenance. She probably had you working nonstop."

"You were right about that, but I'm no longer working for Samara."

"She fired you?"

Lydia shook her head no. "I quit."

"Good for you."

"That remains to be seen," she uttered in response. "I need to find a job now."

"You will," Jasmine stated firmly. "Working for Samara Lionne was just a stepping-stone. It's time for bigger and better things."

Their food and drinks arrived.

"So tell me, did you meet any handsome cowboys in Montana?" Jasmine asked. "Or did Samara keep you too busy to even notice the opposite sex?"

"Actually, I did meet this one guy, but things didn't work out between us," Lydia confessed. "I guess we were just too different." She tried to sound nonchalant.

"That's too bad."

She changed the subject by saying, "I'm really glad to be home."

"Why don't we do something together this weekend? Let's have a girl's night out."

"Sounds good to me." Maybe going out with Jasmine would help to take her mind off Wesley and her broken heart.

"Are you okay, Lydia?"

She nodded. "I'm fine."

"You must have really cared for this guy."

"I did . . . I do," she confessed. "I love him."

"So, tell me about him," Jasmine

prompted.

"He's tall, dark and handsome," Lydia began. "Wes is rugged in a cowboy kind of way. He's unlike anyone I've ever met. The night we met, my knees were weak the whole time. I'm not sure how I was able to even dance with the man. I even got on a horse for this man."

"What?"

"He took me on a cattle drive. We went on a wagon ride through the Wild West and even went mining." Lydia smiled. "I found some garnets that I'm going to have set in a bracelet for my mother. Wes and I spent a lot of time together talking about our plans for the future . . ." Her voice died as she realized all she had lost.

"He sounds wonderful."

"He was, or so I thought," Lydia stated. "Wes and his wranglers are no longer a part of my life."

"What happened between you two?" Jasmine inquired.

"I don't really want to talk about it right now. It's too painful."

Her friend nodded in understanding. "Why don't we do something later this evening? We can have a nice dinner and then see a funny movie."

Lydia smiled. "I'd like that."

She didn't want to stay home too many nights alone. Lydia did not want the ache of loneliness to sink in and take root.

"I was surprised to get your call," Samara said as she joined Wesley at a table in the hotel restaurant. "How are you?"

"I'm confused by everything that's happened," he responded. "I was hoping that we could clear up a few things."

She smiled at him, but Wesley didn't believe that it was sincere.

"Sure. What is it that you want to know?"

The waitress arrived, putting a temporary halt to their conversation.

"I'd like a pitcher of iced tea and two bowls of the house salad," Wesley stated.

Samara did not seem fazed by his ordering for them both. She was probably not used to doing anything for herself anyway. He knew that Lydia took care of the actress's daily needs even though she was in Granger and Samara was in L.A.

"Why the ruse?" Wesley asked. "Why did you go through all of this trouble? Surely it wasn't just to purchase my land."

"This was not about you, Wesley. Not really. I found something I wanted and I went after it . . . discreetly, of course. You really shouldn't take this personally — it's done all of the time to protect the privacy of the high-profile buyer."

He met her gaze straight on. "Then what or who is this about?"

The waitress returned with the pitcher of tea and two glasses. She served them both before disappearing again.

"I sent Lydia here to do some research for me, as you already know." Samara took a sip of her tea and nodded in approval. "I wanted to keep my identity a secret because I didn't want the media to get wind of my plans."

"Did Lydia know that you were planning to buy property in Granger?"

"No, she did not," Samara responded. "I didn't inform her of all of my plans. It's strictly on a need-to-know basis."

The woman reappeared with their salads.

Lydia had been telling the truth. Wesley felt like a heel over the way he'd treated her.

"She wasn't lying to you," Samara stated as she placed her napkin into her lap. "But you were too full of yourself to believe her."

"Excuse me?"

"Even after the way you treated her, Lydia chose to honor you by no longer working for me. She quit the very next day. She was the best assistant I've had."

A part of him was relieved that Lydia was

no longer working for Samara. He didn't think she truly enjoyed working for the actress. "I don't think her leaving your employ had anything to do with me. Perhaps it was all your doing."

Samara shrugged in nonchalance. "It really doesn't matter anymore."

"Why did you buy my ranch?"

"Because it was for sale and it fits my needs," she responded.

"I get the feeling that this is not really about the ranch. I don't know what you're after, but I will find out," Wesley told her.

Samara laughed. "I'll invite you over once all the renovations are completed. You and the rest of your family. In fact, I plan to invite the entire town."

"I thought you were seeking a place for solitude."

"I am," she stated. "Doesn't mean that I don't want to get to know my neighbors."

He was getting nowhere with Samara. "I just don't get why a woman like you would be interested in living in a town like Granger. I would think that you'd be more comfortable in a place like Los Angeles."

Samara gently wiped her mouth on the edge of her napkin. "That's because you really don't know anything about me, except what you've read in the tabloids." She laid down her knife and fork. "Wesley, don't you think you should reserve judgment until you get to know me? After all, look what's happened with you and Lydia."

Lydia clicked on the send button. She had done that at least ten times within the past hour. Job hunting was not something she relished, but it had to be done because Lydia enjoyed having a roof over her head, food to eat and bills paid. She had been able to save some of her earnings, but it was not enough to carry her long-term.

Maybe I shouldn't have been so hasty in quitting.

No, it was the right thing to do.

A wave of hurt washed over her as an image of Wesley materialized in the forefront of her mind. As much as she wanted to blame Samara for what happened, Lydia could not.

It was completely up to Wesley to choose to trust her and he refused. Her mood veered to anger. This was a man who seemingly cared for her. Lydia was angry with herself for loving him. Despite all that had happened, she loved him still.

It doesn't matter, she told herself. Wesley hadn't tried to contact her since her return to L.A. She had not bothered to call or email him, either. Lydia believed that it was all for the best. She could never forgive him for the way he treated her.

Lydia knew that there was a possibility of Samara going after Wesley. She felt deep down that her former employer harbored feelings for him. What other reason would she have for wanting to know so much about him?

She didn't think that he would fall for someone like Samara, but then there was a time when Lydia never would've believed that he'd cast her aside so easily, either. Or that he would break her heart.

Wesley Broward was clearly not the man she had thought him to be.

"You've been pretty quiet lately," Jameson noted as they unsaddled their horses.

Wesley gave his brother a sidelong glance. "I would think that would please you."

"Laney told me that Lydia left town."

"She did." He was careful to keep his expression blank. Wesley did not want his brother to see how much he ached for Lydia.

"You may not see it right now, but maybe it's for the best," Jameson stated. "Sounds like she played you, man. I heard that her boss purchased your ranch in Hastings."

"You're wrong," he countered in return. "Samara Lionne played me."

"She couldn't have done it without Lydia's help, though."

"I thought the same thing, but then after a conversation with Miss Lionne, it became obvious that Lydia had nothing to do with her plan to purchase the ranch. I just hate that I didn't realize this earlier."

Jameson studied his face for a moment before saying, "You really love her, don't you?"

"I do," Wesley confirmed. "Not that it matters much now. Jameson, I really messed up. I jumped to conclusions because I was scared that you might actually be right, but mostly because I was afraid of what I felt for Lydia."

"Wesley, from what I'm hearing, there's only one thing you can do to make this right," Jameson stated.

He eyed his brother. "What's that?"

"Go get your woman. If Lydia means this much to you, then you can't just let her walk out of your life. Go after her."

Wesley broke into a grin. "I'm going to do just that. I need to take care of something first. After that, I'm going to Los Angeles to get my woman."

CHAPTER 18

Lydia gasped in surprise. "Wesley, what are you doing here?"

She could not believe that he was in Los Angeles, but what did it mean? Lydia was still hurt by the way he had treated her. She reminded herself that she could no longer trust him with her heart.

He had come after her, but it was too late.

"I had to come, sweetheart," he responded. "My life has not been the same since you left Granger."

"I can't do this. . . ." She needed more time away from him to ease the pain. "You have to leave, Wes."

"I was wrong, Lydia," he blurted without preamble. "I'm sorry and I hope that you can find it in your heart to forgive me."

She shrugged in resignation.

"Do you still love me?" he questioned.

"Yes," she responded softly. "I love you, Wesley, but this doesn't change anything between us."

"Honey, it changes everything. We belong together."

"You don't trust me, Wesley," she responded. "And a relationship can't work without trust. You and I both know this."

"I wouldn't be here if I didn't trust you. I made a huge mistake and overreacted. I'm sorry for hurting you. Right now, I need you to trust me. Trust that I will never intentionally hurt you."

Lydia met his gaze.

"You aren't the only one who has had to deal with trust issues, Wes. I have my own demons to deal with when it comes to trusting men, but I opened myself to you." Her eyes darkened with pain. "After my father walked out of my life, it was hard to trust anyone, but then I met you. I thought . . . finally, here is a man who really loves me."

"I do," Wesley quickly interjected. "I love you more than my own life. Lydia, I can't stand being without you, sweetness. I've been walking around with a big hole in my heart since you've been gone."

"You really hurt me, Wes."

"I'm sorry. If you give me another chance, I'll spend the rest of my life making it up to you." His broad shoulders were heaving as he breathed. "I don't want to lose what we have." Wesley sighed heavily, his voice filled with anguish. "I don't want to lose you."

Lydia chewed on her bottom lip as she considered his words.

"What made you change your mind?" she asked.

"I had a conversation with Samara," he told her. "She told me that you kept our relationship a secret and that you didn't know anything about her plans to move to Montana."

"The thing is that you shouldn't have needed to hear it from her, Wes. You should have trusted that I would tell you the truth."

"You're right," he admitted. "Lydia, I'm not a perfect man. I made an error in judgment, and I'm trying to make this right."

"I appreciate you coming to L.A. and telling me this, but it really doesn't matter anymore."

"What do you mean that it doesn't matter?" he wanted to know. "Lydia, what we have is real. How can you just give up so easily?"

"I wasn't the one who gave up," she countered. "It was over the moment you thought I'd betrayed you."

"No, it wasn't, Lydia." Wesley lifted her face so that she could look into his eyes. "You left Granger instead of staying and trying to work things out. I was angry initially, but we could've gotten through it together," he said in a low, tormented voice. "You are angry with your father for the way that he walked out of your life, but you did the same thing to me."

Lydia hadn't thought of it that way, but she couldn't deny that Wesley was right. She had run away without trying to work things out with him.

"I love you," he said tenderly.

"Wes, I'm sorry for leaving the way that I did. It's not like me to run from a fight, but at that moment, I was so hurt that I didn't know what to do. I realize now that I should have handled it in a more mature manner."

"We should have talked it out."

She agreed.

"So what happens now, Lydia? Are we really over?" His steady gaze bored into her in silent expectation.

"I love you so much, Wes."

He pulled her into his arms.

Wesley's mouth covered hers hungrily.

The kiss left Lydia weak and burning with a deep desire. She clung to him, holding on for dear life.

His hands moved gently down the length of her back. "I've missed you so much, honey."

"I missed you, too."

"What's in the boxes?" Lydia inquired. Wesley was carrying them when he arrived. At the time, they were not important.

"Open them and see," Wesley responded with a smile.

She burst into a short laugh. "You bought me a pair of cowboy boots. Wes, I love them."

"Now open this one," Wesley instructed.

"A cowboy hat. . . ." She broke into a grin. "How did you know that I wasn't going to ask you to leave?"

"I wasn't sure," he responded honestly. "I hoped and prayed that I could convince you of my love."

Lydia set the hat on top of the box it came in. "We have a lot to discuss, Wes."

"I know."

"The first of which is how long do you plan to be in town?"

He smiled. "For a week."

"Only a week?"

Wesley nodded. "I have to get back to work, I'm afraid. I was actually hoping that you would come back with me, Lydia."

"I'm not working right now, so I guess I could."

"I want you to come back for good," he announced.

"Are you saying that you want me move to Montana?" Lydia asked. His hands lightly traced a path over her skin, making it hard for her to think.

"I'd like that, but if you want to stay here in Los Angeles, then I suppose we can come up with some sort of compromise. We can spend half of our time here and the other half in Granger."

"I don't mind living life on the ranch, but I do have my own dreams."

"I understand," he responded. "As you already know, there are other things that I'd like to explore, as well."

She noticed that Wesley was staring at her. Lydia tried to assess his unreadable features but was unsuccessful. "You're doing it again."

"Doing what?"

"Staring at me," she responded with a smile.

"It's because you're so beautiful and I never tire of looking at you. I thought I could do the whole long-distance thing, but not seeing you . . . Lydia, I can't do it. I want you with me."

"It's been a struggle for me, as well," she confessed.

He reached for her, pulling her close once more.

Explosive currents raced through Lydia as he captured her mouth.

"I want you," he whispered.

She moaned softly.

Wesley swept her, weightless, into his arms. "Where is your bedroom?"

She pointed and he carried her down the hall. He walked through the door and placed her in the middle of the bed.

Wesley crawled in behind her.

Lydia could feel his uneven breathing on her cheek as he held her close. The touch of his hand was almost unbearable in its tenderness. His mouth covered hers as he kissed her passionately.

The touch of her lips on his sent a shock wave through Wesley's entire body with a savage intensity. He planted gentle kisses on her shoulders, neck and face. As he roused Lydia's passion, his own need for her grew stronger.

Passion pounded the blood through her heart, chest and head, causing Lydia to breathe in deep, soul-drenching drafts. She had never been as happy as she was in this moment, and she didn't want it to end.

Lydia knew that she wanted to be with Wesley forever. This was the man she had always dreamed of — he was the one she loved unconditionally. He was the man God created to be her life partner. Her soul mate.

As they united in love and ecstasy, Lydia vowed to give her heart to no other man for all of eternity.

Wesley wasn't sure what the future held for him, except that he wanted Lydia in his life forever. He vowed to wait as long as it took for her to regain her faith in him. He loved her dearly and was not going to give up on what they shared.

He watched the rise and fall of Lydia's chest as she slept, thinking about what transpired earlier. She made him feel loved in the way that she touched him, kissed him and responded to his touch.

Wesley placed a protective arm around Lydia, pulling her closer to him.

She moaned softly but never opened her eyes.

He planted a kiss on her lips and then lay back down and closed his eyes.

They slept for almost two hours.

Lydia woke up first. She eased out of bed and tiptoed into the bathroom to turn on the shower.

She jumped when the door opened.

"Are you planning to shower without me?" Wesley asked.

"You were sleeping," Lydia responded. "I

didn't want to wake you."

He moved closer to her until they were touching skin to skin. Wesley was extremely conscious of where his warm flesh touched her. "I'm awake now."

She gave him a seductive grin. "Care to join me in the shower?"

"I thought you'd never ask."

After a longer-than-usual shower, Lydia and Wesley navigated back into the bedroom wearing fluffy towels.

Wesley picked up his shirt and reached into the pocket. "I have something for you."

Lydia laughed. "You bought me a cowboy hat and boots. What can you possibly give me now?"

He pulled out a small black velvet box.

Wesley bit back a smile at the look of surprise on Lydia's face.

He sat down beside her on the bed. "Lydia, will you marry me?"

Wesley opened the ring box.

Her mouth dropped open, but no sound came out.

"Honey," he prompted.

Unshed tears glittered in her eyes. "You had the sapphire set in a ring?"

He nodded. "I thought it would be the perfect engagement ring for you because I know how much you love them. When I found it in that pail of dirt, I knew that we were definitely meant to be together."

She smiled. "It is definitely the most perfect ring for me. Wes, it's stunning."

Wesley agreed. "But it will look even better on your finger. However, I can't give it to you until you answer my question. Will you marry me and make me whole?"

Lydia met his gaze. "Yes, I'll marry you."

Tears rolling down her cheeks, she held out her hand for Wesley to slip the ring on her finger. Lydia admired her ring. "It's so beautiful. I love it."

She leaned over and kissed him. "And I love you."

Wesley exhaled a long sigh of contentment. "I am a happy man."

Lydia snuggled up against him. "I can't wait to tell my mother. She's going to be thrilled to hear that she's getting a son-in-law." She glanced over at him. "How do you think your family's going to take our engagement?"

"They will be happy for us, Lydia."

"Even your brother?" she inquired.

Wesley nodded. "He actually encouraged me to go after you. Jameson knows how much I love you."

"We're talking about your brother, right?"

He laughed. "Yeah. If anything, take it as

a sign that we are definitely meant to be together."

"I suppose you're right."

Wesley reached over and loosened her towel. "Enough talking for now, sweetness."

She stretched and yawned, waking Wesley.

"Hey, darlin'," he mumbled sleepily. "What time is it?"

Lydia glanced at the clock on her nightstand. "Six o'clock."

Wesley shot up in bed as if he had just discovered he had overslept. "I can't believe I slept so late."

"We did not do much sleeping, remember?" Lydia reminded him. They had spent much of the night making love.

Wesley smiled at the memory. "Oh, yeah . . ."

"Why don't you go back to sleep?" she suggested. "I'll make us some breakfast."

"Come back to bed," he requested.

"Wes . . ."

He planted kisses on her forehead, her cheeks and neck, sending delicious spirals down her body.

They made love once more.

An hour later, they were dressed and in the kitchen.

"You don't have to do anything," Lydia

told Wesley. "You're my guest."

"I'm not a guest," he countered. "I'm going to be your husband."

Lydia pushed him out of the kitchen while she prepared breakfast for them.

"I have to be honest with you, Wes," Lydia said as she prepared the ingredients for southwestern omelets. "After giving it some thought, I'm not so sure I want to go back to Granger to live. Especially since Samara is planning to make her home there."

"That's fine," he responded. "We can stay in Los Angeles, if that's what you really want."

She looked up at him. "It's not fair to ask you to just leave your family and everything you love in Granger. I keep thinking about your house and how much it means to you to live in the house your great-grandfather built."

"I appreciate that, but what is it that you really want to do?" Wesley asked.

"I'd still like to open my own entertainment management firm one day," Lydia responded. "I really believe it's something I'll be good at."

"Then we will do whatever is necessary to make that happen, sweetheart. If you can handle Samara, then you can deal with anyone, in my opinion. Hey, I'll even help you."

His words thrilled her. His support meant the world to Lydia. "You really mean it?"

Wesley nodded. "I will support you in whatever you choose."

Lydia broke into a smile. "I really love you, Wes."

"I love you, too, darlin'."

"In the meantime, since I don't have a job, why don't we travel to Europe and see some of the places you've dreamed about visiting?" she suggested.

"I actually like that idea," Wesley responded. "What do you think about going to France first?"

"Wherever you go, I will follow," Lydia told him. "My place is by your side."

"The cowboy and his lady," he murmured. "There's a new chapter to the Broward story — the one we will create."

"I have the perfect name for it," she stated as she set a plate in front of him. "Wrangling Wes. . . ."

ABOUT THE AUTHOR

Jacquelin Thomas has published more than fifty books in romance, women's fiction and young adult genres. When she is not writing, Jacquelin enjoys spending time with her family, decorating and shopping. Jacquelin can be reached at jacquelin thomas@yahoo.com. Visit her website, www .jacquelinthomas.net.

The employees of Thorndike Press hope you have enjoyed this Large Print book. All our Thorndike, Wheeler, and Kennebec Large Print titles are designed for easy reading, and all our books are made to last. Other Thorndike Press Large Print books are available at your library, through selected bookstores, or directly from us.

For information about titles, please call:
    (800) 223-1244

or visit our Web site at:
    http://gale.cengage.com/thorndike

To share your comments, please write:
    Publisher
    Thorndike Press
    10 Water St., Suite 310
    Waterville, ME 04901